D0933484

FOR SALE BY OWNER

For B.J. and Monte

And for my grandparents,
Margaret Hanna Bobrovcan and John Bobrovcan,
together since 1943.

FOR SALE BY OWNER

stories

Kelcey Parker

Kore Press ▯ **Tucson** ▯ **2011**

 **Kore Press, Inc.**
Tucson, Arizona USA
www.korepress.org

ISBN: 978-1-888553-55-0

Design by Sally Geier
Cover design by Lisa Bowden
Art Direction by Lisa Bowden
Type is set in Baskerville and Bell Gothic BT.

We express our gratitude to those who make Kore Press publications possible:
The Tucson-Pima ArtsCouncil, The Arizona Commission on the Arts,
through appropriations from the Arizona State Legislature and the National
Endowment for the Arts.

TABLE OF CONTENTS

And whatever it would be to me — this life that other women seem to be so — happy in; this feeling that other women — have — to offer to the man they —

— Elizabeth Stuart Phelps, *The Story of Avis* (1877)

DOMESTIC AIR QUALITY

Thank you, in advance, for participating in this market research study. The information you provide will be used solely for the purpose of creating new products to enhance the quality of air in your home.

Monday, February 16
Journal Entry

Dear Tammy and Lydia,

I realize that this is supposed to be corporate and anonymous, but I prefer to address this journal directly to you. As a young girl I always gave my diary a name. For a while she was Jewel, a glamorous substitute for my own dull Jill. That was first grade when, every few months, I carefully unlocked the gilt-edged cover to report about the weather and various holidays. Later I had a Hello Kitty notebook and I called it Kitty and began every entry, Hello, Kitty! The exclamation point was an upside down teardrop over a big fat heart, and I spent most of my entries apologizing for not writing more often. But then I learned that Anne Frank also called her diary Kitty, and I didn't want to end up like her, so I settled on the usual Dear Diary. Soon enough, I came to think of Diary as a name, and she, Diary, became a persona not unlike my previous trustworthy, sweet, pretty, Platonic-ideal-of-myself confidantes. So it is either ironic or inevitable to find myself here: a pregnant thirty-two-year-old mother of three, writing to "Tammy and Lydia" about the quality of air in my home for $300.

Our house, as you know from your visit, is a new house in a new neighborhood, and I believe even the air is new. In fact, this may turn out to be a non-interesting study for you because air quality seems to have been a top priority when the house was built last year. If we were still in our old house, I'd have all sorts of things to say about the moist, moldy air in the basement, about the drafty windows, the food backed up in the unreliable disposal, the funky wafts drifting our way from the Chinese carry-out around the corner, the sounds of REO Speedwagon's *Hi-InFidelity* from our neighbor's garage (are such offenses not covered by the Air Quality Act of 1967?), and the general smells of three kids, two adults, two cats, and one terrified hamster living in a two-bedroom house.

But now we are in the Big House. We moved here last summer, thanks to Nate's hard labor and to the promise of continued low-interest rates that would keep his small mortgage business thriving. Our son Jack had just turned one last year when Nate started talking about having another child, a little buddy for Jack since the twins had each other. But the five of us were already crammed into the two bedrooms of our house, the girls in one room and Jack and his crib in ours, and the last thing I wanted was another child in that house. I wasn't even sure I wanted another child. Plus, I thought of *myself* as Jack's buddy, and I wasn't eager to give up that position. He's always been a Mama's boy, serious and shy, preferring the company of adults to that of other children.

Anyway, the next thing I knew, we were meeting with the Zaring people, choosing our floor plan, customizing our interior, and adding upgrades: yes to granite countertops, yes to crown molding, yes to finished basement with walkout, yes to Jacuzzi in master bath, yes to landscape with retaining wall and Japanese water garden a.k.a. goldfish pond, yes, yes, *yes!* The next thing I knew after that I was pregnant.

Prompt: Read each of the following words, one at a time, and write down the first words or phrases that come to your mind.

Rain—Love Reign O'er Me.
Sunshine—You'll never know how much.
Kitchen—How's about cooking something up for me?
Bathroom—I have four of them.

Wednesday, February 18
Journal Entry

Dear Tammy and Lydia,

You might think that because I didn't say much about air in my last entry or because my word association was a bit irreverent that I'm not concerned about air quality. And you would be right. With the exception of the first few months of any pregnancy, when every strange smell sends me running to the toilet, I don't usually think about the air in my home. I admit that when you both came over last week to tell me about this study, I began to feel like I should've been more aware of something as important as air quality. You mentioned the adverse effects of poor air quality—allergies, illness, irritability, fatigue—and I, unaware, uninformed, felt accused. *J'accuse!* It was a maternal failure: how can one protect her children when she doesn't even pay attention to the very air they breathe? It is, as you said, like not noticing the weather—not providing your child an umbrella for the rain, no mittens for the snow. But then, as you conceded, your comparison broke down because your whole point was that, whereas the weather is out of our control, we can—we must!—change the air quality of our home.

I appreciate your prepared speeches and checklists and pamphlets ("Fifteen Fun Facts About Air!"), I do. Knowledge is power, and I am now armed with the knowledge that millions upon millions of pollutants and toxins and germs might or might not be, but probably are, floating around my house and struggling to slip past my children's nose hairs. I'm just not always sure, as a mother, what to do about such knowledge. All the other moms keep talking about growth hormones in cows that are going to cause my milk-drinking, hamburger-eating children to start puberty at age six. Between the air toxins and the growth hormones, it feels like the Communists battling it out with the Nazis, and my house is the tiny Eastern European country.

So, Tammy and Lydia, I'll do this for the $300 and because I enjoy participating in market research studies (a bit too much, if you ask my husband), and I promise to provide you with detailed, accurate, and up-to-date information on my domestic air quality three times a week as agreed upon. But I do take issue with the fact that your company, P—& G—, insists on creating problems and needs where there are none. Or not many. Or different ones.

The current conditions—to return to the assignment—are acceptable. I just changed Jack's diaper and gathered up a basketful of dirty clothes. The diaper is in the Diaper Genie, which was a gift and is a pain to use, but clearly my using it reflects an intrinsic desire to ward off unpleasant air. (Doesn't it?) The clothes are currently being washed with the Mountain Breeze version of a detergent put out by your competitor.

Prompt: List the top ten sources of unpleasant odors in your home.

The bathroom after Nate gets home from work; laundry piles scattered like land mines; Nate's golf bag, especially his glove; the cat litter when Nate forgets to change it; the kitchen garbage full of half-eaten eggs, cheese slices, and bananas; Nate after he works out; food under the high chair; the bed when Nate's too tired to shower after he works out; the clothes in the washer that get moldy when I forget to move them to the dryer; Nate's clothes when he thinks I don't know he's been smoking; sex.

Friday, February 20
Journal Entry

Dear Tammy and Lydia,

Just a few days into this and it occurs to me that I no longer think of "Tammy and Lydia" as *you*. Though I just met you a week ago, I'm already forgetting what you look like. Lydia is older, shorter; Tammy younger, taller, leaner. Lydia has teenage children, Tammy has none. (Tammy had an engagement ring—tiny, princess cut—but no wedding band.) Lydia: bleach blonde hair with a Dorothy Hammill cut on round face; Tammy: long, brown, possibly permed hair, with thin bangs. Is this right? Does it matter? I mentioned before that my old diary entries were always addressed to some better version of myself, and now, as I think of "Tammy and Lydia," I can almost picture two optimal selves, which, it turns out, can pretty much be divided along the same lines as the women in my book club.

There's the Lydia camp: These women are married with children, and afraid their brains are starting to show the same results of disuse as their thighs. Oprah books, classics, and *Reviving Ophelia* are their mental girdles. But, alas, they are the first to wrap up the evening—cued by a subtle signal exchange that I, though one of them, have yet to catch—and hurry home to relieve their husbands, who probably still have not been able to get the kids to bed.

And the Tammy camp: These are the never-been-married women who want to find out what a shopaholic might confess or just why the devil wears Prada. A pair of shoes on the cover is required.

I had hoped that moving into the Big House would help me feel more like the Lydia I am, but instead it's made me more acutely aware of how far I've come from the Tammys, or have always been. Of how much bigger my house, my marriage, my kids are than me.

So, Tammy and Lydia, this is why I have to picture you both as I met you last week: Lydia in your corduroy skirt, cream tights and loafers. Tammy with your dark blue skirt, striped blouse and fake pearls. Each of you reminding me that I need to get my act—my domestic air act—together.

Prompt: Put a check beside no more than three of the following words or phrases that best describe the air in your home.

	Fresh	√	Still
	Unhealthy		Inviting
	Moist		Dry
	Stagnant		Fragrant
√	Clean	√	Other?

Please describe:

I don't even notice that there is air in the house. It's like when a window is so clean you think it's open until you smack your hand against it. Scary.

Monday, February 23
Journal Entry

Dear Tammy and Lydia,

Last week I was still trying to get used to thinking about air quality, but today I can tell you that I was very observant about odors and moisture and temperature and overall quality this weekend, and I have much information to report. First off, and this is an objective fact, not a judgment: my family stinks. I hadn't really noticed it before because this house is so big and I'm not what you would call a regular cleaner, but things can hide just as stealthily in the space here as they did in the clutter of our old house. The truth is that Melinda and Miranda wear the same socks and underwear for too long, then they leave them under the bed or in the hallway or shoved in a closet, each emitting a subtle stench. They are like little anti-air-fresheners, un-Plug-Ins. There are the discarded sippy cups with milk that curdles and molds. The Diaper Genie is less effective than it proclaims. Moreover, Nate, who has been working late (in the middle of the month, dear?), neglected to change the cat litter—one benefit of being perpetually pregnant: it's not "safe" for me to change the litter—and we got in a fight about it this weekend.

The litter is in the basement, where we don't have to smell it, but the cats do have to smell it, and Nate knows that if he forgets to change it, the cats will stage a protest and pee in a strategic spot. Sometimes it's the bathroom rug, sometimes a laundry pile, and they have even used our bed. But this time, one of the cats (I'm pretty sure I know which one) got into Jack's crib and used *it* as a litter box. Usually we grab both cats and rub their noses in it like they're dogs, like they care. But their choice of Jack's crib seemed a personal offense, and after I rubbed their noses in it, I called Nate into the room. I pointed into the crib, and as Nate bent over the railing to try to figure out what he was supposed to look at, I put my hand on the back of his head and shoved it down. He jerked up.

"What the hell?" he said.

"I just thought you should see the cat's new litter box," I told him.

Nate is a big man with thick shoulders and a kind, full face that charmed me into marrying him a half-dozen years ago. He has the same football-player build as in his high school pictures (with just the slightest expansion), a friendly Irish face with fair skin, a few freckles, greenish-speckled eyes, and a warm personality that other women adore and that I occasionally do not. His eyes, large and unsurprised, looked into mine and narrowed. He opened his mouth as if to say more, then he just shook his head and walked out of the room.

I'm rambling on a bit because the girls are at preschool, Jack is asleep, and all around me are chores to put off. Anyway, Nate cleaned the litter box that day, and I washed Jack's sheets and made dinner. This brings us back to air quality. The dinner—baked, seasoned chicken with potatoes and gravy and corn—filled the house with a delicious aroma, and I thought of your words, Tammy and Lydia, "Air quality affects everything." And you're right—you don't even realize it. At least not until you do a study like this. The bad air made the cats protest, and it made me mean to Nate, and the savory air of dinner brought us all to the table where everything was forgiven.

> *Prompt: Ask someone who has not been in your home all day (your husband, your mother, a friend) to tell you the first five words or phrases that come to their mind as they enter your home and inhale the air. Identify the person's relationship to you and list their words here.*

(T & L, a quick note, call it Quality Control: You've got plural pronouns—they, their—referring to singular nouns—someone, person. There's no need to be sloppy just because you're dealing with stay-at-home moms.)

I didn't ask Nate because he doesn't exactly know about this particular survey. He thinks that moving into our Big House means, in part, that I shouldn't do market research studies anymore. It seems we now have an image to maintain. I didn't ask my neighbors because I don't particularly want to invite more comparisons of each other's homes; we do this enough as it is. My mother lives three hours away, and my girlfriends and I rarely go to each other's houses because it's too impossible to juggle nap schedules and their work schedules. Anyway, my mother sent me a package with some new clothes for the baby—frilly, pink summer outfits—and so I showed the UPS-guy the prompt, and he said: "nice," "pleasant," "good," "fine," and, when pressed for a fifth, "big."

Wednesday, February 25
Journal Entry

Dear Tammy and Lydia,

Jack puked all over his clean sheets, the leftovers are going bad, and the overall air quality is poor. The girls fought over who had more cereal in their breakfast bowls, and then again over who left the cap off the purple marker, and finally over who would be first to enter the preschool classroom. Jack has a low-grade fever, and is both lethargic and fussy. He seems annoyed at his lethargy, which prevents him from satisfactorily expressing his fussiness. I'm exhausted from waking up with him throughout the night. Even the baby seems too tired to kick around in my belly.

This is all somewhat typical for a Wednesday. In the middle of the week I feel stranded on an island between the comforting shores of the weekend. Not that the weekends are very comforting, but then I'm not alone with the kids, and the air seems different. Nate breezes in like a western wind, and I'm reminded that this is our life, these are our kids—the walls of this Big House did not erect themselves around me, nor did the kids sprout up out of the ground like weeds at my feet. Nate and I did this together, and on weekends (when he is not "working late") he looks around approvingly and declares it good.

So just like our air shields the earth from harmful sun rays and even burns up meteors before they can reach the earth's surface (Fun Facts #11 & #12), there is a protective quality to the air on a weekend in February when Nate is home and when the sun sets early, convincing the children that seven o'clock is a reasonable bedtime.

By the way, I should clarify that I mentioned the baked chicken dinner from the other night because I was especially proud of it, but I can't let you think it's representative. I was doing penance for the thing with Jack's crib. All too often we have spaghetti and frozen meatballs, or tacos, or fish sticks—none of which do much for the air.

Prompt: Describe your favorite season. How does the air in this season differ from that of others?

My favorite season is whenever it's not golf season. For as long as I've known him, Nate has been bad enough at golf to keep it from taking up too much of his time. But as soon as we moved to the Big House last summer, he started to take the game seriously. He used the money we'd set aside for patio furniture to buy top-of-the-line clubs, and justified this purchase by saying that having the best equipment meant he'd spend less on lessons. ("Less on lessons?" I said dryly.) Instead of working late, he's "golfing." Instead of living room furniture, we have an indoor putting green.

Friday, February 27
Journal Entry

Dear Tammy and Lydia,

It's Friday, and things feel better already. You should try to invent some kind of TGIF product that makes the air feel like Friday air. I didn't mean to get so down before, but it *is* fifteen degrees outside, and I *am* in my third trimester. Tonight the Berdings are having a neighborhood cocktail party to liven up the off-season, that dull time between Christmas parties and Memorial Day grill outs. Unfortunately, I can't share in the cocktails, but it will be fun to get out. It gives me a reason to wear my one nice maternity outfit, and going out always reminds me of how much I like Nate. He has the charisma of a frat-boy with the good sense not to pledge. He's a lot of fun at parties, and we used to go to them all the time, but that was back in the stone ages, B.C., before children.

Back then we swore we would keep up a schedule of going out on dates and having "couple" time even after we had kids. It would be as easy as dropping off the baby at Nate's parents' house and enjoying the evening. But what with separation anxiety and pumping bottles of breast milk and how early his parents go to bed, not to mention that they were *twins*, you can imagine how well that worked.

Now at the Big House, we are all somehow versions of people we hung out with in high school, catching up on old times. We can all come together over drinks on a Friday night and have a good time as peers. In the summer, my twins ran around the yard with neighbor kids, and with Jack trying to catch them, until past their bedtime. Nate and I drank Coronas with lime (before I knew I was pregnant) out of a cooler, sitting on lawn chairs on the driveway—as if the sidewalks were sidelines to some sporting event—with the Berdings, the Hamiltons, and Jeff Faber (Barb rarely comes around). Nate in his element: generous, handsome, funny, and sure.

Despite Fun Fact #1 ("We cannot see, smell, or taste air"), the air on those nights was vivid and delicious. The green smells of the freshly cut grass and the equally freshly cut lime; the muted sounds of all of our kids laughing and shrieking, letting us know they're not too far away and they're happy; the light sprinkle of air bubbles against my upper lip as I tipped back my Corona. And Nate. Nate offering a bottle of beer to everyone who walked by on their evening stroll, making jokes about giving one to the neighbor's baby or offering to pour some into a bowl for the dog. Everyone smiling and laughing, and we feeling worthy of living here in this Big House, where the air is so clean and healthy.

Prompt: What is the most inviting space in your home? What makes it more welcoming than others?

The painting in the foyer. Our foyer's got a cathedral ceiling, so light pours in from the second-floor window, and it's the only place we've painted so far, a honey gold color that looks great in the light. So that's nice. But over the staircase there's a painting my mother bought us, a giant framed print of a nineteenth-century summer picnic where all the members of the town come out in their brightly colored outfits. The old men playing checkers in the background are the same size as the young girls and the horses in the foreground. There are no air toxins or growth hormones and everyone is always happy. That's where you want to be.

Monday, March 1
Journal Entry

Dear Tammy and Lydia,

So it turns out that parties are a lot less fun and my husband is a lot less charming when I'm sober. The Berdings' house filled quickly, and I could see the quality of the air change and decline as if it were in Technicolor. At first, the front door opened often enough with new guests to allow for a cool, dry burst of air to relieve my lungs and my head. But the temperature and moisture increased in proportion to the volume and the open bottles, as did my headache. I started to feel faint. When I was pregnant with the twins, I nearly passed out on a number of occasions. My head would empty of blood, my vision would darken, and I would fumble into a chair and scavenge for some crackers. I've experienced this less with Jack and with this baby, but Friday night I felt like I was fighting for air and space. I could practically see all of the carbon dioxide being emitted into the room as more and more people arrived and talked and breathed. I looked in vain for some plants to counteract it, to make some oxygen, and I became convinced that global warming was occurring on a smaller scale, at a more accelerated pace, right there at the Berdings' house, and that by morning we'd all be found dead.

Nate was entertaining one group or another, while I begged pardon for my belly as it bumped against someone everywhere I turned. I ate because I could not drink, and within an hour I was sick from the Swedish meatballs, the cheese rolls, the crab dip, the artichoke spread, and the pesto pitas. I slumped into an overstuffed chair, feeling sick to my stomach, faint, fat, hot, and sober, while Nate exerted a great deal of energy in the telling of a story (the firework accident—he tells it every time), gesturing with one arm, while the other held a nearly empty beer bottle and rested lightly on Mary Gehring's shoulder. I know he's not attracted to Mary (certainly not when there's cute Christie at the office), and I know that he feels sorry for her living with those three big dogs since her husband left, but to watch Mary sip her glass of red wine and beam her red teeth up at Nate while I sat alone in an overstuffed chair as described above, was really too much.

I focused my attention on my belly, feeling around for the baby's head and butt to see if I could get her to play our little game where I poke her and she kicks back. She ignored me too. I was wondering if this would be typical of our relationship, and I found myself lecturing her in my head: *Young lady, you had better learn to listen to your mother*, etc. But I know how kids are about being lectured, so I dropped that for another approach: *If it weren't for you, I wouldn't be here right now.* But this sounded off the mark because even though I was having a miserable time just then, what I meant was more of a revelation: that we wouldn't have moved to the Big House if we hadn't decided to have another baby, and that I actually preferred to be at a bad party in our new neighborhood than isolated in our old, crowded house. I began to back-peddle (*What I mean is...*), but I felt very peaceful just then that she *did* know what I meant and that I didn't need to explain myself, and this made me feel bad about the fact that I hadn't really wanted to get pregnant again, and that I hadn't really wanted another girl. I wasn't sure I should bring that up, but there was something about how peaceful and patient she seemed—like she had all the time in the world and like she also knew the party was a bust—so I told her I was sorry for any negative thoughts and that I would prove it by making her the best nursery, which I also apologized for not having started (or even thought about) yet.

I was considering room colors and patterns when my thoughts were interrupted by a loud crash, and I looked over to see Nate on the floor surrounded by a circle of laughing neighbors. This wasn't the first time he'd overdone the shirt-on-fire part of the story. Hal Berding grabbed his forearm and pulled him up. Mary Gehring was the first to get a napkin for the small amount of blood oozing from his brow. The Berdings' pet Labrador, who had been lying against my leg, jumped up and—I'm convinced, for the air turned more sour—farted. Then he (she? it?) nuzzled his wet nose into my palm, and I rose, wiping the dog snot on the microfiber, and bellied my way to Nate. I took the wet napkin from Mary Gehring, handed it to Nate, and announced that it was time to go. The crowd sighed and booed in its drunken, jolly way, but also respectfully parted as I led Nate to the coats in the study and then out the door.

The outside air was so fresh that it burned my eyes. But my head felt clear and empty. I was glad Nate had hurt himself—though how or on what I did not intend to give him the satisfaction of inquiring—because it saved me from staying any longer and from haggling over when to leave. I thought I felt the baby give a little kick, a sign of allegiance, though that very well may have been the Swedish meatballs.

"Son of a bitch," Nate said, touching the napkin moistened by Mary Gehring to his forehead.

Walking home, the winter night was big enough for our tension to spread and dissipate like a snow that doesn't accumulate, but even our Big House was too small and close with the Ralston girl babysitting and bearing witness, and the atmospheric pressure felt low and heavy. Nate tried to steal away to our room, but I had to stop him for his wallet, and that simple exchange took more effort than either of us had to give, and we didn't manage to pull off even that in front of Becky Ralston with her sleepy eyes and anxious smile.

The rest of the weekend, Nate used the kids to avoid me, taking them to a matinee and then leaving them at his parents' house to "catch up on some things" at the office. I channeled my frustration into cleaning. Long story short: the house has never been cleaner, the air never better.

Prompt: Please identify what you believe is the best product you've purchased that improves air quality. Describe what makes it so effective for you.

That *Febreze* is like a miracle potion; ever since I started this study, I've been spraying it on my clothes, my bed, my furniture, my carpet. Maybe I should dab it on my neck or wrists to see if it works on my husband.

Wednesday, March 3
Journal Entry

Dear Tammy and Lydia,

The clean house charmed Nate and last night he was all snuggles and sweetness. He lifted my T-shirt and talked to the baby about all the fun we were going to have as a family and about what a great mom she was going to have. This in lieu of an apology; I admit it worked. He sweet-talked his way up to my chest, where I let him remain for a time. I liked the feeling of his body against me and the baby, and I hoped she would give him a good kick. I put my palm on Nate's shoulder and traced the line of his collarbone with my thumb until my hand was cupped around his neck. I gently lifted his face and held it inches from my own. His lips glistened with traces of saliva, but it was not his lips I wanted to see. I wanted to look deep into his eyes for a reason not to worry. And I wanted him to see my eyes—to see my worry, to see a warning. But Nate's expression was as dazed and blank as Jack's always was when pulled from my breast.

"I'm worried," I said.

I felt pressure against my hand as if Nate had determined that any worries I had could be discussed with his mouth at my nipple, but I strengthened my grip on his throat.

"No, Nate," I said. "Listen to me. I'm worried."

He shifted his body off of mine and propped his head on his hand. "Okay," he sighed. "About what?"

Was his exasperation real or feigned? Was he a man with nothing to hide, just trying to share an intimate moment with his wife? Or was he already on the defensive, trying to deflect and belittle any sign of concern? I pulled my shirt down, clasped my hands together over my raised belly and stared at our ceiling light, at the dark silhouettes of dozens of dead bugs.

"Forget it," I said.

Prompt: Browse your favorite home magazine for images of ideal environments. Choose one that is especially pleasing to you and describe it here.

I don't have any home magazines.

Friday, March 5
Journal Entry

Dear Tammy and Lydia,

I can't get comfortable. My back hurts, and the temperature is all wrong. I turn up the thermostat and I sweat; I turn it down and shiver. But I don't have a fever or a subtemp. I took a bath after the kids went to bed last night, and I want to take another one. I feel like one of those people who can feel the weather changing in their arthritic joints.

The kids are watching *Clifford*. Next up, the announcer says, is *Berenstain Bears*. Mary Gehring just came by. She let the kids pet her giant slobbery dogs and made sure to tell me about a date she has tonight (translation: she's not after my husband). I let her say what she needed to say, then closed the door and told the kids to wash their hands.

No, Mary, I thought, it's not you I'm worried about. Cute Christie has twice your looks and more opportunity. Plus, living in an apartment on her secretary's salary, Cute Christie is much more impressed by Nate's Big House. (He gave her a personal tour when we'd had all nine employees over last Labor Day weekend.) And having never been married, she's taken— ironically but unabashedly—with Nate's image as a devoted family man. But right now it's not Cute Christie I'm worried about either.

Prompt: Place a check beside no more than three of the following words or phrases that best describe the odors you would most like to have in your home.

√	*Rose Rain*	√	*Potpourri Explosion*
√	*Ocean Breeze*	√	*Cupcake Cream*
√	*Apple Medley*	√	*Pine Passion*
√	*Citrus Zing*	√	*Chamomile Country*
√	*Cinnamon Bread*	√	*Spring Bouquet*
√	*Lavender Lilacs*	√	*Sea Spray*

Tuesday, March 9
Journal Entry—Additional Insert

Dear Tammy and Lydia,

Outside the window, amid the dry brown landscape, one premature tulip is trying to turn itself upright. A reminder that even though you can't see it or feel it (rather like air in this respect), inside the earth's belly, spring is moving and stirring, eagerly waiting to be born.

Inside my belly, on the other hand, is nothing. Because my baby is dead.

Which is why I said to Nate, "I'm worried, I don't feel right, take me to the hospital," even though I knew. This is the kind of knowledge that must be deferred as long as possible. Hope and denial—which I'd lived with for days, or longer—are better by far.

I ask myself now: what is knowledge to hope? to denial? Now I know all I need to know about stillbirths. One in every 150 deliveries is a "still" baby. Two-thirds of stillbirths are the result of "undetermined or unknown" causes. Still babies may be organ donors. And I'd just as soon know nothing at all.

She stopped moving. Like my other babies, her movement started in about the fourth month—a push here, a roll there—and gained in frequency and intensity over the next couple months. Then, like a bag of popcorn in the microwave, the kicks just slowed down, then slowed more, and then stopped. All weekend I pressed my hand against her and took baths to try to jolt her, but by Sunday night, I could no longer avoid the truth. I tried one final bath at two a.m., but nothing. *Nada y pues nada*. As I reached out to nudge Nate's shoulder, I couldn't help but think, *You very well may deserve this*. But I wasn't sure, and I needed him probably more than ever at that moment, so I touched him lightly.

"Nate. Honey." I said.

At dawn, Nate got the kids up and took them to his parents' house and me here to the hospital. It was confirmed right away. They did an ultrasound and couldn't find a heartbeat. They were sorry. I said I was tired and ready to go home. They said they were getting a room prepared for me. I said for what. They said for the delivery. The delivery? I said I'd rather keep her right where she was, safe inside me. They said they were sorry but that wasn't possible. They said my room was ready.

So. They induced labor and I spent the day reading pamphlets between contractions. Loss Before Life. Grieving for Your Stillborn Child. The brochures were so poorly written. They were vague ("stillbirths are as random as raindrops"), ridiculous ("stillbirths are an equal opportunity destroyer of dreams"), and presumptuous ("when a baby dies, a bit of our future is erased before ever being written"), but I found myself touched by the fact that someone had bothered to write and print them at all. One pamphlet (Grief is a Process) suggests writing in a journal as a way of expressing emotions. So here I am, Tammy and Lydia.

She was so tiny and perfectly formed. Perfect, except—according to preliminary autopsy reports—her lungs. I held her in the crook of my arm, her cheek to my swollen chest, hoping that the smell, the touch of my nipple against her skin might trigger that involuntary reaction of turning and sucking, just as her presence caused my breasts to burn and fill. I held her all through the evening, letting her go only for Nate or my mother (she'd made the drive) to hold her, or—per the recommendation of the March of Dimes—for her picture to be taken, her footprint to be made.

I talked as if she were alive, as if she would come home and grow up with us.

"She's a fiery little one," I said. "She'll hold her own with Jack and the girls."

And she would have. She had Nate's fair complexion and the down of her hair shined red in certain lights, but she had my eyes. Even though I had to open and shut them with my fingers—no matter how much I silently prayed for her to do it herself, just once—and even though they had the gray-tint of newborn eyes, I could tell they were mine.

"I think she's going to be our little athlete," I added. For Melinda and Miranda are not interested in sports, and Jack already shows signs of becoming something like a research assistant. I began to see clearly how this little girl would be an anchor for our family, how she would both ground and surpass our other children, how she would give me motivation and clarity as a mother.

"She'll be at the top of her class," I said, kissing her forehead.

They should suggest this in their pamphlets: "Pretend there's nothing wrong, that your child is alive, that your life will go on as originally planned."

By midnight my baby's skin (she has a name, I cannot write it) had grown cold and they came to take her away. I let my tears fall onto her face, and I touched the wet salt into the skin of her eyelids—one last hope in magic.

Now it is Tuesday morning, and I am alone with an empty belly in an empty room. My milk has come in (something, alas, is full), and they have given me a pump to release some of the pressure. Nate has gone to get breakfast and to bring more of the kids' clothes and toys to his parents. I have to tell you, Tammy and Lydia—on this hospital notepad—that the air quality is not satisfactory. My gown smells of dried blood, my breast milk is already going sour, the food is processed and stale, and chemicals drip all around me. This is not a healthy environment. But the doctor has just checked on me and assured me that the air is fine, that I can still have more children, and that it was not my fault.

> *Prompt: If you could live anywhere in the world, where would you live? Describe your ideal environment, paying special attention to details of air and climate.*

Wednesday, March 10
Journal Entry

Dear Tammy and Lydia,

This morning they discharged me from the hospital, and Nate took me to his parents' house to see the kids. I held them all tight and cried, wanting to take them back to our house. But Nate and I had to go to the funeral home because "state laws assign parents responsibility for the disposition of their stillborn child's remains." Disposition? Tammy, Lydia, do you know what that means? It means: 1) *somebody's usual mood or temperament.* So we are responsible for the mood of our daughter's remains. Or, 2) *the settlement of a legal matter.* Her remains, then, are the legal matter. Or, 3) *See "disposal."* In which case we are responsible to throw her away.

At the funeral home, we spoke with a nice woman—a human pamphlet—skilled in the art of channeling people's grief into productivity. She gave us things to do, decisions to make. Where would we bury our daughter in relation to our own plots? What time of day would work best for a ceremony? Would a graveside ceremony suffice, or would we prefer a church? With which church were we affiliated? Who else needed to be contacted? Were we interested in upgrading the casket quality for a mere $200? What kinds of flowers would we like? Lilies were recommended to cover odors. It's good to know someone is thinking about air quality.

Prompt: Suggest one new air-improvement product you would like to find on the market. (Note: According to the terms agreed upon for this study, any ideas listed below become the sole property of P—& G—.)

I think I have an idea.

Thursday, March 11
Journal Entry

Dear Tammy and Lydia,

I've been watching television all afternoon. The funeral was this morning. It was just a small thing, more of a memorial service. I don't know what to call it. I insisted that we take the kids home afterward even though Nate's parents offered to keep them another night and even though I just sit in front of the TV ignoring them. The girls are sad because they looked forward to being the older sisters of a sister. And Jack is sad because he doesn't understand why his mommy is sad.

The answering machine is full of kind messages. The kitchen desk is full of unopened cards. The refrigerator is full of expired milk, limp vegetables, leftover containers, casserole offerings, and their respective foul odors. Full. Full. Full.

The television is full of products dedicated to air quality. Fruit-smelling tablets to put in the garbage disposal. Deodorizing garbage bags. I never would've come up with those. But as that little casket was lowered into the ground, I thought about the air-quality in the coffin. It had seemed like a healthy environment when we chose the cushioned pink satin interior, but now I'm not so sure. The dark wood, the dirt, the lack of ventilation all seem very poor indicators. Tammy and Lydia, is there something you can invent to improve the air quality in a coffin? Some circulation system? I worry about my little girl

Prompt: List all products you purchased in the last year that were specifically designed to improve domestic air quality.

Scented candles, a Plug-In that dried up and wasn't replaced, a houseplant the cat ate and threw up all over the carpet. Oh god.

Monday, March 15
Journal Entry

Dear Tammy and Lydia,

According to Fun Fact #9, "the air pressing down on your shoulders weighs about one ton, but you do not feel it because you are supported by equal air pressure on all sides."

I respectfully disagree. I feel every single pound.

I know, I know. It wasn't Melinda or Miranda or Jack that died. The baby didn't live to be two—a life full of surgeries, transplants, and complications—and *then* die. She wasn't my only chance at children, or at having a girl. She wasn't even, the doctors say, my *last* chance at having children. And everyone who has come with flowers and food for which I'm grateful, really—reminds me of these things to make me, or them, one of us anyway, feel better. And then, though the wound is fresh, they can't help themselves. They inhale, pause, scrunch their pity face. They say, "So, do you think you'll have another?" They quickly add, "Not right away, of course." Of course.

"I don't think," I tell them.

Even Nate can't help himself. He wants to know the same thing. (How else to get through the now?) Do I think we can have another?

I can smell his breath when he asks this. He's been eating the lasagna someone gave us.

"I don't think," I tell him.

I don't tell him that when I *do* think I wonder about his fidelity and whether all of this has been some sort of divine judgment. Or that I also think about air quality for a market research survey. I don't tell him that I have learned that no matter how many products I buy or *P—& G*—makes, air, which we can't live without for more than five minutes (Fun Fact #6), by its very nature causes corrosion and decay.

Nate tells me he doesn't mean right away. Of course. "But I just want to know," he says.

I thought I wanted to know if my baby was okay, but I was wrong. There are things I thought I wanted to know about Nate.

"There are some things I'd like to know too," I tell him.

He furrows his brow, shifts uncomfortably.

When I look deep into his eyes that won't quite hold my gaze, I see all I need to know.

I smile. "But what is knowledge," I say, "to hope? To denial?"

I am thinking of these as the primary elements of my existence—hope, denial, air—when Nate accuses me of being cryptic.

I apologize.

I tell him, yes, we can have another child.

We can have everything.

Of course. Of course we can.

I reach out and take his unshaven face gently into my hands.

Then—like a child about to eat a cooked vegetable, or maybe about to drown—I take a deep breath of the air in our Big House, and kiss and kiss him.

BEST FRIEND FOREVER
ATTENDS A BABY SHOWER

The Hostess: lemon meringue. Blonde hair like egg whites—whipped, frosted, baked—pulled back in a ponytail that curves around her pearled neck like a scabbard. Smooth butter skin. Yellow zest cardigan with a delicate cable knit. White pants holding firm to a well-toned gluteus. Curiously absent panty lines. Less curious considering that she works in fashion. (Even the Best Friend Forever, who doesn't know a thing about fashion, knows that panty lines are unfashionable.) The Hostess is sooooo glad everyone could make it. Almost as many ooooo's as are polka-dotted pink and yellow on the Chinese take-out party-favor boxes.

The street is a secret. It doesn't fit even into a local's understanding of the neighborhood's geography. The Best Friend Forever lived in her first apartment less than a mile away and never even knew it existed. Fifties cape cods surround and protect the enchanted haven like soldiers, like a moat, like a decoy. Perhaps a fairy tale character founded it on one of those woodland adventures. She was not eaten by a wolf or a witch: she planted magical seeds that grew into four-bedroom, three-bath imitation Tudors with in-ground pools and three-car garages.

Like the Vatican: its own country.

With its own aristocracy. The house belongs to the Hostess's mother, queen monarch. Next door lives the Hostess's sister and the future of the line. A dozen other homes—over half of the street—are owned by various relations of the Hostess.

I know, she says. Isn't it sick?

But the Hostess positively hates that she has to live two hours away for work right now. She comes home every weekend and can't wait to take her proper place on the street when the time comes. The time clearly *should* be coming soon. She's almost thirty now, she tells the Best Friend Forever without quite making eye contact (she is busy assembling a truffle garden on a plate), and her thirty-one-year-old sister, who is pouring drinks at the counter, is way ahead with five—five! she repeats—years of marriage and two—two!—small children.

But apparently the Hostess's triumphant return to the street is not coming so soon. The Hostess, her mother, her older sister, and now another younger sister—they simply keep multiplying, multiple platinum!—glance at each other and share a knowing, sad smile.

Screw Jimmy, one of them says. Or was it Timmy?

Screw himmy, the Best Friend Forever agrees, raising her plastic cup of champagne punch to show her allegiance.

The four women stare at her, each a different shade of blonde.

Hugs and warm smiles from the Mom-To-Be, whose belly is as flat as ever, whose baby is somewhere in China.

The Best Friend Forever is introduced to the Mom-To-Be's fashion coworkers, who all work for Calvin Klein or Kenneth Cole, as the oldest and dearest friend.

We've been friends, the Mom-To-Be says, since we were, what? Five? (The correct answer is four.)

The Blonde Nobility and the other Fashion Guests blink and nod like dummies (ventriloquist dummies, of course) then whisk away the Mom-To-Be.

Chunky shoes feel like cement blocks amid the delicate taps of a roomful of stilettos. Are fairy godmothers still in the business of conjuring glass slippers? One can always hope, especially when one is left alone in the kitchen with a polka-dotted plate of stuffed mushrooms, salami rolls, and off-limit truffles. The Hostess's mother returns momentarily to take a plate of brie and crackers to the other room. She smiles sympathetically at the Best Friend Forever, who does not appreciate being interrupted from her slippery line of thought.

Brie! The mother says brightly—an exclamation and an explanation—and disappears again.

Salami! The Best Friend Forever calls back, holding a salami roll like a cigar.

The Mom-To-Be is heard in the next room discussing baby names. Decision by committee. Her primary criterion is that the name be *different*. But a long time ago the Mom-To-Be didn't want to be different. She wanted to be the same as her Best Friend Forever. She wanted to wear the exact same terrycloth outfits and have matching water guns as they played Prince Charles' Angels, fighting crime with their best Lady Di accents.

The Best Friend Forever has an urge to call out to the other room, Name her after me! I'm different! If only to make the point that being different pretty much sucks.

But the quiche is ready!

The Hostess instructs the group to choose a spot in either the dining room or the kitchen and to bring a plate to get served. The Fashion Girls head to the dining room with the Mom-To-Be; the Blondarchy move toward the kitchen. Chunky shoes go for some more of that yummy punch and follow the Mom-To-Be, who seems so unlike herself amid her retail co-workers. When did she become so fashionable?

Paper lanterns hang from the chandelier. Fortune cookies sit atop the polka-dotted (ooooo) take-out-box favors. The quiche is tepid (ha!), but no one dares say so. Fresh fruit. Pinafores.

The Hostess pours coffee from a silver teapot, offers a choice of General Foods International creams. Then she insists on refilling the empty water glasses, which is good because chunky shoes would attract negative attention clomping into the kitchen, but which is weird because last the BFF checked, this was not a restaurant.

Then one of the Fashion Girls says, Let's read our fortune cookies!

It is not worth pointing out that fortunes are to be read and cookies are to be eaten.

Fashion Girl A: *Hell is paved with good intentions.*

That's weird, everyone agrees. Another Fashion Girl hesitantly suggests that she thought it was *the road to hell?* But then she shrugs. She must have been mistaken.

Fashion Girl B: *You are going to get some new clothes.*

Everyone—almost everyone—reaches for the fortune, but Fashion Girl B holds it safely behind her back, smiling.

Fashion Girl C: *Never wear your best pants when you go to fight for freedom.*

All: That is sooooo true. (S-polka dot, polka dot, polka dot, polka dot, polka dot.)

Mom-To-Be: *You are filled with life's most precious treasure—hope.*

All: Ohh! How sweet! It's perfect!

The Best Friend Forever, who would like to bang her head against the wallpapered wall, has *You have heart as big as Texas*, but decides this is a poor translation. Retranslates for the Fashion Girls: *Confucius say, the greatest danger could be your stupidity.* The Best Friend Forever does not always behave as well as she should. Especially when left alone with unlimited champagne punch.

Around the table it becomes unclear whose stupidity is being referred to. Perplexed eyes blink and glance at familiar fashion for comfort. The Mom-To-Be flushes. It sounds for a moment like someone mutters, *bitch*. But that person is scratching her shoulder, so perhaps it was something about an itch?

The Best Friend Forever decides she better change the subject: So, what does T. J. Maxx have in store for us this season?

Suddenly she is surrounded by a table of manikins.

Then one of the manikins speaks, and so must not be a manikin after all. Jesus, we don't work for T. J. Maxx. That's a retail chain, not a designer.

My name's not Jesus.

And we don't work for T. J. Freaking Maxx.

Sorry. J. C. Penney?

It is about to be attack of the killer manikins when the Hostess reappears and diverts everyone's attention with chocolate-covered strawberries, sprinkled with powdered sugar. The tray is passed around the table, and the Best Friend Forever selects a strawberry for herself, feels the tickle of powdered sugar in her nose, and sneezes all over the remaining strawberries. When all the eyes at the table double in size and settle their focus on her, she does it again.

Where I come from, she says to the mutes, the proper response is, Bless you.

It is time to open gifts!

No, no, no, put your plates down, the Hostess's younger sister says. We'll totally get them later.

The Hostess's older sister sits on a large pillow. Her skirt, daisies with gemmed carpels, fans out like a picnic blanket for her miniature gentleman, the only male allowed. Everyone fawns over the suited young man, except for the BFF who ignores him simply because if he were twenty years older he would ignore her.

Gifts are opened: bibs, Baby Einsteins, layettes, designer outfits, *three* ear thermometers. (Oh my god! No way! Three?) There is an uncertain pause when the Mom-To-Be opens a handmade gift: a painting of the Chinese symbol for love. She gasps and holds it before the group as she warmly thanks her Best Friend Forever, who takes another long sip of her drink. Why do they serve it in such dinky little cups? It's almost gone again.

The Fashion Girls and the Blondistocracy study the painting, unsure what to make of a handmade gift, especially by a strawberry poisoner.

Are they impressed, or do they think it's pathetically sweet, like a child's attempt at cursive? Or like Tiny Tim's version of a Christmas present? The painting is passed around and there seems to be some interest, some forgiveness for the sneeze. You made this? Do you paint a lot?

Yes, the Best Friend Forever painted it. She paints a lot. Hiccup. It was her major.

Attentions, though, are deficit, and the subject switches to the Mom-To-Be and her upcoming trip.

So, when do you hear about your baby? When do you go to China? How long do you stay? What do you have to take?

Next week will be six months from the file date, so she hopes to hear soon. They'll get a picture and find out the approximate age of the baby. She and her husband will fly to China four-to-six weeks from then. They have to pack everything for the baby—diapers, formula, bottled water, clothes, blankets. (The Best Friend Forever didn't know any of this.) They have to bring their own toilet paper because many places lack indoor plumbing.

Here the Mom-To-Be is interrupted. What does she mean they don't have indoor plumbing? Where will she go to the bathroom?

The Mom-To-Be, not quite sure herself, explains that she's heard they just have holes of some sort where you go.

The Hostess's younger sister, clutching the gift list she has composed, struggles visibly with this information. The Fashion Girls squirm and frown. Then the younger sister flips back her hair and articulates what everyone is thinking: Doesn't it just make you sooooo glad that we live in America?

(S-polka dot, polka dot, polka dot, polka dot, polka dot.)

The Mom-To-Be mentions that she wants to bring pictures of her chocolate Labradors to introduce them to her daughter before bringing her home. She doesn't want the baby to be afraid of the dogs.

Why? One Fashion Girl asks. Don't they have dogs in China?

Yeah—for dinner! Answers another.

You're going to have, says yet another, like total culture shock.

With which everyone agrees.

Someone else says, Don't they name the years after dogs and other animals over there? She has seen it on the placemats at Chinese restaurants.

The Mom-To-Be nods and says that this is the Year of the Rooster. Her daughter was born the previous year: the Year of the Monkey.

The Monkey? Weird.

Oh, and don't they have like a Rat year too?

Gross.

The babies will all have two important days: a birthday, if it's known, and a "Gotcha" date. The Mom-To-Be is glad she has dark hair because she has heard stories of Chinese babies rejecting new blonde or redheaded mommies. The blondes nod gravely. They would feel the same about a dark-haired child.

The Mom-To-Be has also heard of babies rejecting parents based on smell.

Someone suggests that she eat Chinese food and not shower for, like, ten days before she goes to get the baby.

The Mom-To-Be has heard other tales of Chinese women approaching American couples and offering their babies in tears. Urging them, in Chinese, to take their daughter to America.

A Fashion Girl tells the Mom-To-Be that she is sooooo unselfish. (S-polka dot, etc.) I mean just think of what a terrible life you're saving this little girl from.

As everyone nods—except for the Best Friend Forever, who wants to save herself with a refill of her drink—the Queen Blonde tells a story of an Asian girl adopted thirty-some-odd years ago by a family down the street. The BFF returns with a full cup and catches the ending wherein the adopted woman now lives in Florida, is an anesthesiologist, and has four children of her own.

The Hostess blinks back her happy tears (it must have been quite a tale) and announces, No more sad stuff—it's time for our game!

The group is instructed to identify the correct nursery rhyme.

Clumsy kids who go to a well.

Elderly woman with unique living quarters.

An aging monarch who likes to smoke, eat, and listen to music.

One of the Fashion Girls says she wants to hang out with that monarch, and all agree.

Small seated girl who is afraid of insects.

It is not worth pointing out that spiders are not insects, but the Best Friend Forever does so anyway.

What are you talking about? A non-blonde replies.

Spiders, the Best Friend Forever repeats, not sure how else to explain.

They're not insects.

The non-blonde glares as if the BFF has just sneezed on a tray of strawberries. Who said anything about spiders?

How about can we just keep going? The hostess says, eyebrows up, nodding like a dreamed up Jeanie. We still have a few more. Oh, here's a good one! *Male trio who bathed together.*

The room is silent for a moment before everyone laughs. Order is restored.

Tired shepherd boy with a trumpet.

Triplet felines who can't keep track of their winter clothes.

The Fashion Girls copy off of each other. Reminisce about cheating in high school. Defend their ignorance on the grounds that they don't have children yet.

The Best Friend Forever has other ideas about their ignorance. She opens her mouth to say so, but catches the eye of her friend, the Mom-To-Be, who smiles at her almost secretly, like she did in those days long before she became a Mom-To-Be, and the Best Friend Forever finds herself smiling back at her own Best Friend Forever instead.

The answers are read.

How many people got all of the answers correct?

Hands and eyes are down.

How many only missed one?

Chunky shoes shift uncomfortably.

How many missed two?

Three?

Four?

Five?

Me! A Fashion Girl chirps, pops up her bangled arm, and is rewarded with a set of three matching candles, which everyone agrees is really too cute.

The game over, the room gets louder, and the circle formation of the group collapses as the stilettos cluster toward each other, surrounding the Mom-To-Be. They can't wait. They're so excited. Oh my god.

Is it over? Can she leave now? The Best Friend Forever and her chunky shoes clomp away, wander in search of jacket and purse, half expecting to be stopped by a guard on an off-limit corridor. But no one is upstairs. The spring jackets are piled on a bed like glamorous, lifeless bodies. The one on top is off-white linen. She picks it up and puts it on.

She can see only her torso in the dresser's mirror because she is too tall. The sleeves—most sleeves—are too short. She takes off the coat and picks up a light madras trench, which does not quite fit at her shoulders. What bothers the Best Friend Forever the most—as she takes another coat and tries it on—is that the orphan baby is almost one year old and may not even have a name. She would never admit it to the Mom-To-Be, but she came across some Chinese words when she was looking for ideas for her painting, and found one she liked for the baby: *Xiu*. It means Elegant. The Best Friend Forever says it aloud, *Xiu*, pronouncing as best she can (though her mouth isn't working so great after the drinks) into the disinterested air of the perfectly perfect room.

She tries another jacket, spins around like a pro. Sort of—a little wobble. *Xiu*. Baptized months ago by the tears of a mother, maybe even a father, she'll never meet, the orphan baby knows only a rotating series of hands and distant bodies. She will be matched to the parents-to-be, not by a strange code of DNA and chromosomes, but by astrological signs and animal years. What a system!

Maybe they'll accidentally match her to the Best Friend Forever.

A silly and impossible thought, to be sure. A fairy tale wish. But hadn't it—or something like it—been there all along, dampening her palm, unsteadying her brush, the whole time she painted the Chinese symbol for love in shades of rose pink and sage green to match the shabby-chic nursery. (What ever will the orphan baby think of shabby chic?) The Best Friend Forever would tell the orphan every orphan story she knows, and the orphan would know she will live happily ever after.

The Mom-To-Be and her laughing fashion friends can be heard faintly, and the Best Friend Forever is feeling, in someone else's jacket, pretty fashionable just about now. There's really nothing to it. She plants her arms akimbo, throws her hip to the side. Ouch. Was that a rip under the arm? Alas, it cannot be overcome: fashion hurts. Stilettos are painful, thongs are painful (lord knows she tried), and size 4 jackets don't fit. The Best Friend Forever will return home, like Cinderella after midnight, and she will not delude herself that anyone would care to find the owner of the chunky slipper.

But perhaps—she puts on a cropped leather blazer, which actually, could it be, seems to *fit*—perhaps she has the wrong idea with Cinderella.

Goldilocks. (Was Goldilocks an orphan? Cinderella was half an orphan. Goldilocks was blonde.) Goldilocks knew how to get what she wanted. The Best Friend Forever eyes the mirror, strokes the soft lilac leather jacket. This one's just right.

When the Mom-To-Be was a kid, she was insecure, almost ugly. She felt sorry for everyone who suffered. She wrote notes and passed them faithfully. She always added something encouraging at the end, like a Chinese fortune: *You are beautiful inside and out. You will succeed in everything you do.* She expressed her love generously. She didn't merely Luv Ya Like a Sis or draw a heart swollen with implants. She signed her notes with a straightforward *I love you.* She was easy to love back. She will be a good mom. The orphan will live happily ever after.

But maybe it isn't possible to be Best Friends Forever, as originally planned in the wee hours of the night on the living room floor eating Bugles and chocolate donuts, twisting French braids, and marking one another's backs with dot dot dots and question marks. Maybe they used the wrong punctuation marks. Instead of ellipses and questions marks, they should have traced Morse code warnings and exclamation points: There's no such thing as forever!

The Best Friend Forever finds a purse and applies someone's lipstick. It is red and fashionable. Even its name is fashionable. *Hot Tomale!* There is a travel-size perfume; she dabs it on her wrist. Another purse! She dumps out birth control pills, cigarettes, receipts for lots and lots of clothes. The Mom-To-Be lives in another world now; the Best Friend Forever dwells in the periphery like the Cape Cods at the outskirts of this enchanted land. It's tempting (as she brushes on someone's Mauvelous blush, which nicely accents the lilac jacket) to want to rescue her old friend from fashion. But it's just as tempting, in its own strange way, under the drowsy power of punch, to want to crawl under all these fashionable jackets and hope that, like the orphan baby, someone will find her and take her home.

Here they come now.

WHAT LIPS MY LIPS HAVE KISSED
AND WHERE, AND WHY

My garden blooms all winter. Rose petals bleed on Northern Indiana snow. Jalapeño and Hungarian hot peppers scythe from stems; their juices numb my gums like Novocain, like a very long kiss. I should not eat them so.

I confess: I stole the flowers. Who would notice an absent hollyhock in a curbed island of Walmart's parking lot. Or a chrysanthemum plucked from the mulch of an optometrist's outdated office.

What they notice is a garden that still blooms in January. Heads sprout over my tall fence like cabbage, eyes bulge like blackberries. Such ripe curiosity in the dead of winter! A lake effect of looking!

"They're fake," I lie to the neighbors as I nuzzle into my parka and spray plant poison like fertilizer. "Happy New Year!"

؎

It was autumn when I gave Kenneth one of my library books. "Here," I said, pressing it into his open palms, "take it."

My account has been closed for years, and when I try to view my activity online, a loud siren goes off and my cats mew and mew. So I no longer try to find out how much I owe in fines. I just take what I want.

Sometimes I hide between the stacks and strip away the electronic tag. Other times I twirl my bag of books over the sensor as I exit. I wear blue pumps and smile like Mary Tyler Moore. No one is suspicious of an English teacher at a library, even if she never seems to check out any books.

Kenneth clutched the book in his hands and thanked me. He's the kind of kid that knows the difference between a used book and a used sweater. He held the used book like a bomb that needed to be diffused, thrust it under his used sweater, and ran out into the rain.

The next morning he awoke after uneasy dreams to find himself transformed into a giant insect.

His mother blamed me.

"Prove it," I said.

The local news portrayed me as young and attractive because it made the story, their story, more salacious, but if I really were young or attractive, I would have captured the attention of the national news: followed by the Fox, pursued by the Peacock, surveyed by the Silver Eye. In addition I would be happily married.

Over winter break with no students around, the janitors trade porn in the boiler room and smoke cigarettes by the delivery gate out back. They don't even notice me.

I unlock my classroom with a spare key they haven't confiscated and stand before the chalkboard. Yesterday was a lecture on *Lolita*. Our city's library, I explained, was the first to ban the book from circulation despite the fact that no one in charge of decision-making had read it. This is how the world works, I said.

The day before was a poem analysis, Edna St. Vincent Millay's Sonnet XLIII. I explained how to calculate Roman numerals: X is for a kiss; L is for the lonely tree; III is for me, me, me. Then we discussed the where's and why's.

Today I write on the board: COURSE EVALUATIONS. I put a copy on each desk and say, "There is reason to suspect that the previous evaluations were tampered with, so you are being asked to complete them again. Please check the appropriate box for each question. Be as honest as is necessary. The future of my career should have no effect whatsoever on your response." Then I add: "Nor should any rumors you may have heard."

I am organized and well-prepared. I seem to enjoy the materials and the class in general.

Strongly Agree, Agree, Disagree, or Strongly Disagree?

One by one the evaluations are completed. The whole procedure goes quite smoothly and this time the responses are overwhelmingly in my favor. I submit them to the superintendent.

"It's too late," he says, dropping the strongly agreeable stack on his desk. "You're already fired."

"I strongly disagree," I say.

I send him a bouquet of roses from my winter garden.

"A job is a job is a job is a job," I write on the card.

�

In my living room is a large thermometer that shows how close I am to bankruptcy. Each day the mercury level rises even as the indoor temperature continues to fall. And even though my heat has been turned off and every night is a three cat night, I begin to sweat. Outside, it is snowing. Outside, my garden thrives like late July.

In the morning I bundle up and grab my power tools. I increase the height of my garden fence and drill peepholes. Five dollars for five minutes. Twenty dollars for a toothpicked sample. Fifty for your very own winter fruit, flower, or vegetable.

In this way, I get the heat turned back on. I don't bother about the phone, which has nothing nice to say anymore.

✦

Eventually I make it to the national news. They come to film my winter garden and are pleasantly surprised to find out about the local story. I am two birds killed in the bush for the price of one stone. The reporters high-five one another behind my back. I can see their reflection in an eggplant.

✦

The first time Kenneth came to see me after school it was late September, about a month into the school year. An entire wall of my classroom is windows, and hundreds of students and dozens of teachers, parents, coaches, and bus drivers were within twenty or thirty yards of us. Kenneth and I were two tropical fish in a large aquarium. What I'm trying to say: it was all very public. Until you need someone, anyone, to say, "Yes, I saw the fish. The fish behaved appropriately." Then no one saw the fish or any aquarium.

✦

If a teacher swears her innocence upon her first English edition of

43

Kafka's *The Trial*—aloud, making eye contact in her bathroom mirror—but no one is there to hear her, has she made a sound?
Innocent of what, asks the mirror, and crashes to the floor.

باب

Kenneth's first visit happened to be the day after my boyfriend James broke up with me without having the guts to mention the other girl. Kenneth wanted to know what I thought of his poem. I teach literature, journalism, yearbook. The students come to me.

I create a good atmosphere for learning. I am available outside of class.

Strongly Agree, Agree, Disagree, or Strongly Disagree?

Nikki once gave me a whole envelope of teen angst. Sara wrote a series of haikus about her abstractly abusive boyfriend. Then there was Heather and the pseudo-sonnets. Twenty-four of them in iambic hexameter. Kenneth had never said a word in class. I didn't even know if he preferred to be called Kenneth or Kenny or Ken. I just called him the name on the roster, though it occurred to me at that moment that I'd never actually called on him at all. Now here he was, holding a piece of paper before me like a tribal offering.

And like the chief of a rival tribe who has just suffered a breakup, I gave his paper a skeptical skim. Then I read it again.

It was, he said as if trying out a practiced translation of my tribe's tongue, his first poem.

I looked at him, looked at the paper, looked out the window. The student body flowed from the school like blood from a severed artery. I looked again at the paper, at the careful, deeply pressed letters that I only vaguely recognized from grading his classwork. I could feel the imprint of the letters through the back of the sheet with my fingertips. Kenneth's hands were deep in his jean pockets, his face serious, his dark eyebrows high with hope.

It was, I said, clearing my stuck throat, not bad for a fifteen-going-on-sixteen-year-old.

It was about a garden that blooms all winter.

ஃ

The scientists conduct tests on my garden. They wear white down coats as if they're handling toxic waste. The reporters camp out in the street. The neighbors brave the cold to chat with the reporters about the scientists. When I go to the kitchen to make tea, the lawyers make jokes about they wish their teachers would've given them some "extra help" after school. Yuck, yuck. The cats paw at the pages of the lawyers' books on the dining room table. One lawyer begins to sneeze uncontrollably.

ஃ

"You probably did do it," James says when I run into him at the coffee shop.

I am a good catch. James is an idiot.

Strongly Agree, Agree, Disagree, or Strongly Disagree?

"Did what?" I say. I look around for the new girlfriend.
"What they say you did."
"And what is that?"
"To that boy."
I wait for him to say more, but he just walks away shaking his head. That's when I see the new girlfriend waiting out in the car.
"I strongly disagree!"

ஃ

The only people who want to talk to me are the reporters. Would I like to comment on my case? On my course evaluations? The lawyers tell me not to talk to the reporters. I tell the reporters to tell the lawyers where they can go.

I meet Ron secretly so the lawyers don't know and so the other reporters don't know. It's quite a trick, but I'm no Hollywood star, so all I have to do is wait for them to get lazy. They always do and that's when I meet with Ron in his white van with KNWS on the side. The van has two front seats, and the back is full of equipment. I feel like a spy until I remember I am the one being watched. Still, I survey my house from the front seat, as suspicious as anyone.

Ron is not technically a reporter, he's a cameraman, so he doesn't ask intrusive questions. He just focuses on me steady like a camera lens.

"How can I show people I'm innocent?" I ask him, believing it's a matter of clothing, hairstyle, expression, camera angle. I sit up straight and turn my shoulders toward his seat. The driver's side window is like the frame of a backlit portrait of Ron. My green front door rests on his shoulder like a parrot, and he looks like a pirate. Grrr. "Is this good?" I tilt up my chin to complete my pose. I am wearing a mauve twinset with a high neckline; my hair is in a low bun; my earrings are small and gold. I feel like someone else.

Ron shrugs. "Doesn't matter. By now people have made up their minds. If you look conservative, they'll say it's an act. If you look like a party girl, they'll say of course."

Ron's hair is tousled and his voice is gravelly, especially when he says party girl. He is the antithesis of the combed and coifed newscasters who are always on the other side of his camera. The ones who juggle microphones and note cards, quoting the neighbors like they're proclaiming bible verses. I realize that's what I look like right now in my twinset: a newscaster.

"But you look great," he says, his head moving closer, his voice low, his breath warm on my lips.

I pull back, search his pirate eyes. "Do you think I did it?"

"Did what?" he says, pulling a twirl of hair loose from my bun.

I kiss his lips.

‿❧‿

My house and my face are on the evening news. I am wedged into the corner of my sofa, knees up to my chin like I'm watching a horror movie. I chew my popcorn slowly. My cats prod me with their paws as they seek a flat plane to settle onto. I point at the TV and tell the cats to look. Maybe they'll recognize me. Maybe it will seem as odd to them to see me here and there as it is for me to be here and there. Do I look innocent or guilty? I am not sure whether I am referring to myself on the couch or myself on the TV, whether I have spoken aloud.

I am still undecided when Kenneth's face appears right there on my television, right there in my living room, and I tremble involuntarily. There is a thick black line over his eyes, so I only see his lips, what lips, and I tremble again. The cats pause, alert, and I say to Kenneth, Don't let them cover your eyes. They are trying to blind you, to prevent you from seeing all that your poet's eyes must see. A piece of popcorn dissolves in my mouth and I crunch the frail remaining shell.

If I could talk to him once more I would say your poems are——. I would say take off the blindfold, you must not be afraid. I would say you will be a great poet. I would say be careful, though, because not everyone, hardly anyone, almost no one, will understand. They will jump to conclusions. They will take things literally. They will think a picture of me is me, a picture of you is you. You will be banned and accused. They will not understand what you see. They will not understand a boy who turns into a giant insect. A teacher, her student. A garden that blooms all winter.

Or perhaps I would say something else, something more selfish. Perhaps I would say, Do you think I'm guilty? *Et tu, Kenneth?* And if so, of what, of what?

و

Ron is savvy with his camera. He knows how to change perspective, alter an image, and transform viewers' perceptions. But Ron's subject is the visible world, what can be seen and photographed, and nothing more.

I like this about him. He is not concerned with what lies beyond our vision, with what lies. He is not concerned with what no one saw me do or not do, with what lips my lips have kissed, or where or why, with metaphor. He is concerned with me, here, now.

He kisses my lips.

I kiss him back.

و

The scientists discover a strange substance in my soil. I tell them it's probably Metaphoracline, or possibly Metaphlouride, or, who knows,

Metamorphocite, and they look at me like I'm guilty as hell.

The sneezing lawyer describes a variety of solutions including no contest, plea bargain, and settlement.

"Which will make you go away fastest?" I say.

ﺎﻠﻋ

Spring comes suddenly. The snow melts. The neighbors' tulips rise up like flags at full mast and everyone is patriotic and relieved that nature's cycle is intact. My winter garden withers; the stems and stalks shrivel like witch's feet without slippers. There's no place like home when scientists, lawyers, and reporters, oh my, are gone, when neighbors tend their own gardens, when Ron is with me.

ﺎﻠﻋ

And in my heart there stirs a quiet pain.

Strongly Agree, Agree, Disagree, or Strongly Disagree?

ﺎﻠﻋ

Before they leave, the lawyers tell me I am not allowed to have any contact with Kenneth.

Duh, I say.

But the rain is full of ghosts tonight. It taps a Morse code on my windowpane. Quiet pain. I cannot say what loves have come and gone; I only know that summer sang in me a little while.

Perhaps—I can't help but think—perhaps someday, some year, I'll be out with Ron and the kids, and there he'll be: walking down the street, taking my breath with him.

(*Mommy, Mommy, where did your breath go?* my astute eldest will say.)

Or: he'll give a poetry reading at the library that banned *Lolita*, and I'll sit alone in the back row, clutching his slim volume, listening to the rhythm of his words and voice, his lyrical metaphors blooming in my wintered mind. I'll lack the courage to ask for an autograph, or to say, Hello, remember me, *Et tu, Kenneth*? But when I leave, my heart will be a large brimming aquarium where brightly colored fish flutter and flash.

I HEARD A FLY BUZZ

When I got married. I stood before the crowd in my false virginal splendor, strung like a Christmas tree with the old, new, borrowed, and blue. I looked distracted, people tell me. How could I forget how to talk, my husband wants to know. *I does?* He says. *I does?*

It was the fly, I tell him and everyone. *Didn't you see it?*

We consult the wedding video, but it is grainy, and no, my husband cannot see the fly that captured my eye. But there I am, looking around and around—eyes up, eyes down, following its every zig and zag—throughout the whole wedding.

To prove my case, I tell my husband where the fly would be if he could see it. *Right now,* I point at the screen and say, *he just flew behind the minister's head; okay now he's over by the groomsmen; here I kind of lose him for a second in the stained glass.* This is not helping matters. I can see myself in the video looking at nothing except the ever-moving fly as I somehow manage to repeat after the minister: to have, hold, sickness, health.

Then, on the couch with my husband, I brace myself for the culmination of the vows. Yes, there I am drawing back my shoulders, standing taller, as the fly (which still cannot be seen on the video) is coming closer and closer to me. Do you M------ take thee P----- to be your lawfully wedded spouse as long as you both shall live? I see myself open my mouth and take a deep breath, so I point again at the television and say, *There! Right there, the fly flew straight into my mouth when I opened it to speak!* My husband grabs my arm and pulls it down. We are both silent as we watch me say what sounds like, *I does.* When I try to correct myself, I say it again.

I does? My husband says. He says this every time he thinks about it.

This time I don't bother telling him that it was the fly. That I tried to speak, I really did, but all that came out was the fly's buzz. *Buzz.* Not, *I does.* I also don't tell him how the fly flew straight down my throat, how it has been inside me ever since, how I feel the tense vibration of its wings as it circles and darts about in the cavity of my chest, how it rarely rests, how—when it does—its feet strike like pinpricks to my lungs, how sometimes it becomes agitated and flies in a fury, and how I believe it has laid eggs, and that it and its maggots are feeding, daily, upon my heart.

POSSESSION

Animals

It's what she wants this. Hamster running rattling wobbling Whisper-Quiet ™ wheel, pausing to stare, pausing to shake the blue metal bars, to saw them with her teeth, to twist her head under the water bottle, to fill her cheeks like a satchel for a trip through the tube, to lie on her back and press at the plastic yellow roof with rubber-stamp soft feet. She wants out. Black poop bullets shoot outside the cage. Once she almost died of her own pee fumes in the petting zone. He hadn't cleaned the cage. It was his job. One cat watches over the cage as a mother, another, the other, as a predator.

The turtledove nests in the hanging petunia plant all summer long— sitting, hatching, feeding one then another then another pair of new chicks until they fly one then another then another away. She tried to water the plant but the bird never left just stared so when the hose was pointed. The hanging petunia died of thirst, though it was more like strangulation, strangled dry. The turtledove remained. Devotion he calls it. Exhausting she calls it. You're like that bird he points out, with the kids. Exhausting she repeats. She can't find anymore of the green spots on the plant the nest the home it's all brown, strangled dry, all brown drought. He guides the pace of their swish swish swish on the porch swing Saturday morning the kids watch cartoons. He declares that turtledoves mate for life. Slowly he says it, for emphasis. She rests her head on his muscled shoulder and says that's funny I haven't seen the male all summer except for the time after the first chicks but before the second when he flew in a with a twig and wedged himself between the rim and the underside of his mate's feathers. Oh and after the second chicks but before the third chicks. Ha ha he says and can't help but grab her breast through her robe.

Laundry

He whistles his life through the house. In the laundry room before the water is on his whistling comes down the laundry chute (her favorite-favorite feature of the house) like his underwear. The rest of the melody follows down the chute to her ear she can hear it. She hums along until finally she picks up the words. *Darling when I think about you I think about loooooove. Feel like making.* It's how she knows what he's thinking his whistling.

She smiles but acts surprised later when. *I can't get no.* The Stones usually have something to do with the kids the ingrates though she usually thinks it's her fault too since she's in charge. *Do you know where you're going to do you like the things that life is showing you.* That one worries her. Not just the bad song part. Or the awkward grammar part. How was your day she asks later. The day has sucked. She folds up her own day and puts it away in the drawer so as to wear the remainder of his stiff starchy day with him.

Groceries
It's where she's alone at last at long last no kids no man no phone Kroger. She is queen. Her subjects crowd every aisle and throw themselves at her feet. Take me with you! To the castle! Cook me! Bake me! Mix me! Cut me! Feed me to your children! No! (She says queenly.) I loathe cooking! baking! mixing! cutting! *But please!* (Says a new voice.) Take me! Eat me! No cooking! baking! mixing! cutting! required, HRH. For I am Instant! Yes she says. You will do nicely.

Holiday
Jacko he calls the pumpkin as they scalp dig deep into brains he calls guts. No guts no glory he says. Today his whistling tune is upbeat. He shot a man in Reno. Just to watch him die. This time she joins the whistling though she is not a good whistler though no one listens above the noise of pumpkin guts, *When I hear that whistle blowing I hang my head and cry.* She always finds the sad part of everything. But she smiles at her Disney princess at her cowboy at her Superman as they dig deep reach in pull out squeeze orange guts in fists with glee. Yes she thinks. That is how to live. Always live. The tricks and the treats squeeze them all orange guts white seeds tiny fists ooze out fingers with glee then the oven toast salt eat eat *eat!*

Cup And Saucer
It takes her by surprise this. The black orange day ends the cornucopia day ends, then it happens nothing happens. They will survive on leftover turkey and football. She is going out. It is the Biggest Shopping Day of the Year. She can't be stopped. Don't even try. On the Biggest Shopping Day of the Year she wedges her car into the roads moves slowly in wet cold traffic lights. All she wants not shopping is coffee caffeine café. No baking turkey pies stuffing stuffed. It's there the café that it happens nothing

happens almost.

Centuries do something, roll away open up peel back, what do centuries do. They presently present a present. Wrapped in paper years tied in ribbon months. Cup to saucer with a slight rattle. Hands free now she reaches out pulls gently the ribbon that unties with ease falls to the floor at their feet. Theirs for she is no longer alone; for there's a present. She surveys the wrapping should she rip in with nails make her own hole tear it off fear fears fiercely, or find tape fastened fixed asphyxiated she can hardly breathe and pull back gently like a banana peel like no something else something softer sweeter than even a banana. She opts for gentle for slipping her hand between the layers and sliding up slowly to the fastened fixed asphyxiate tape. To go easy with the years. How many exactly. She thinks she knows what's under the paper years but it's been so many how many exactly years that maybe not. Especially here of all places and on the Biggest Shopping Day of the Year.

But it is. Hello he says from room 46 from Mrs. Mazza's homeroom from another town from. Another life. The life before the one before this one. Or before that. Three or so lives hence. Hello he says again as she contemplates asphyxiates wrapping him back up tying him back up. Yes she agrees unable to do anything not least wrap him or tie him back up. Hello.

It is already happening.

Nothing is happening she says.

Of course not he says.

She eye eye eyes his ring. Thumbs her own. Could it happen something nothing maybe almost now it can. Moments ago there was no it no happening. How does something come into existence out of nothing. Matter comes from matter she learned in the class about physics after Mrs. Mazza's homeroom. Maybe there is no it. No it to happen. Then she will be safe. She will be able to tell the one she married: whoo a blast from the past. She will be able to say it was nothing at all. Say nothing. It was nothing. Certainly nothing that could happen.

But it was happening.

What is happening she says.

He says nothing. Nothing he says.

He is wrong he is wrong to say nothing. You are wrong you are wrong she tells him.

I said nothing he said. There's nothing wrong with saying nothing.

Something was happening she was sure. What was it. Saying nothing is wrong. It is wrong to say nothing when something is very clearly happening. What is the thing she wants to know. What is it.

He says nothing again.

So it was only happening to her.

The sugar crystals on the table could he see them. Or would he say nothing about those too.

Maybe it is not nothing finally he says and she looks from the sugar crystals to his ring to his black lashes. They punctuate his eyes like so many commas so many pauses short short breaths.

Apostrophes, he corrects her. For contraction and for possession.

Oh, she pauses contracts eye eye eyes his ring again. Possession she says of the gold circle and looks back to his apostrophes.

Well he says.

There is gray in his hair and in hers but hers is dyed. If he looks close enough though he will see. Will he. Look. She leans forward across the table he is sitting there now. An apostrophe on his cheekbone she her finger she touches the cheek pushes lightly and lifts away. It his hers black curve on her fingerprint.

It's mine she tells him.

The remaining apostrophes blink at her. What shall you do with it he says.

I shall use it she says to contract (but her own muscles her breath contract like having a baby which is wrong she should contract tiny words which is nothing at all). And to possess she adds when her breath returns.

Obviously he says.

No she says. Not like that. Like this. She holds her finger his apostrophe to his lips. Make a wish she says.

He licks lips inhales eyes close.

No she says! Eyes open.

And he does it he opens looks right at her he wishes he puffs his air it bursts upon her face and Gone! the apostrophe has vanished.

He did it.

You did it she says. She puts both hands around her cold coffee mug. He did just what she told him. What else. What else could she make him do.

Admit it she says. It's happening.

Yes.

You admit it?

Yes.

What else could she make him do.

Take off your ring. Give it to me.

It is large and heavy and possessive but it is in her hand he put it there just like she said. She drops it in her cold coffee. Takes off both of hers women get two and drops them in.

Now you've done it he says.

Tell me your wish.

She's coming he says. She'll be here soon. I need it back.

Tell me your wish she says but he is silent. It's happening she reminds him but it hasn't happened yet.

Not he says yet.

I propose a shift in tense she says. Let's put it in the past. Let's make it happened.

His eyes and apostrophes are on the coffee cup. I shouldn't have he says. I just. She's coming. Soon.

It's unhappening then.

Yes.

Moments ago it was happening and she could make him do anything and. Centuries ago they happened together. Now nothing now. Nothing. He was right after all. But something. How does something appear out of nothing then go away again. Like God. That's what God does.

She takes a long drink fills mouth with cold coffee and gold. Slides tongue through thick gold ring.

The other she arrives. A blast from the past he explains. He greets kisses her cheek and introduces the she's. An apostrophe for a plural. No more contraction possession.

The other she squeezes his hand feels the strangely sticky ring knows she has arrived just in time.

Toothbrush

Whoo what a blast from the past she says later that night. She is good at this tone but she has waited too long to mention it. The right time was earlier when he said did you get any presents today and she said oh yes but had nothing to show for it. On layaway she'd explained. That's how I do it.

And if he ever paid more attention he'd know that's not how she does it. But he pays attention hours later when she mentions a blast from the past that didn't come up earlier.

Oh he says like a question. His eye eye eyes are suddenly on her like spotlights.

Someone I knew in high school she says and shoves a toothbrush in her mouth so as not to say more. She ducks offstage into the closet brush brush brushing.

He follows her and stands close while she brushes. She ducks past him and spits brushes spits brushes spits rinses. Aahhhh she says. He is right behind her and as she turns she says it in his face. It reminds you of how old you are, she says face to face she can hold his gaze, to see someone eighteen one day and thirty-eight the next.

It's not really the next day he says. They are still eye eye eyeing each other as if at a game of poker with lots of chips between them. It's been twenty years he says.

That's true she agrees. Good point.

There is no use in talking about it. Whatever it was that the centuries did whatever came from nothing and became something (it did!) and returned to nothing whatever didn't happen almost happened didn't. (Contraction.) If it were something then that would be different but if nothing happened there was no it and there's no use in talking about anything as nothing as that.

She strips down to. Nothing. Come on she says tenderly getting into bed come to bed. (I am yours she thinks of the one peeling back the covers like wrapping paper. You are mine. Possession without apostrophes. Who needs apostrophes. Who.) It was nothing she says. Nothing she says happened.

MAUGHAM'S HEAD

"It's a matter of getting from here to there, there to here," says the man whose tie points toward where his belly button must be.

The chandelier jingles when he hefts his body and moves the chair, and this makes Maugham think her very large home needs more support and less open space. Why did she agree to a house with ceilings so far away that she can't even reach them on a ladder with a broom, or vice versa? The ceilings are skies and each room is its own country, and the hallways and foyers are oceans and dead seas and sometimes she needs a little something for the motion sickness when she travels from one place to another, from here to there. Sometimes she needs a passport to get from one country to another, and other times she just sneaks over the border when no one's looking, only to find that she doesn't speak the language of its strange overgrown inhabitants. She understood them better before they could speak. Mommy, they used to call her. Now it's *Mo-om*.

But she hears only the new name she has assumed: *Maugham*.

Maugham is placid, unflappable. Maugham is wise: *I have an idea that some men are born out of their due place.*

Maugham is in her dining room now with the man whose tie is a ski slope on the mountain of his belly. She is in her dining room, where the closest anyone has come to dining is circling the table full of holiday appetizers, chairs pushed in so as not to get in the way of the close orbit around the table. The chandelier is a constellation. Now it tinkles like an earthquake rattling in the sky. A skyquake.

"Where do I sign?" she says, knowing there is a place for everything, except for her. You are here.

"Right here," he says. With one hand he is pointing at an X on a paper; with the other he is offering a retractable pen with the company's logo on it. Maugham recalls that this is how she got her oversized house: writing her name beside X after X. You are here. It's partly her fault, if she thinks about it, so she'd rather not, that they're running out of space. If people like her didn't leave perfectly good houses closer in to move to these houses farther out, or have three girls closing in on driving age when they might have had none, there would not be this need for another road.

"A road?" she'd said, pressing fingertips to her temples, when the man had first explained his offer. "In my head?"

"A win-win situation," he'd said.

Now she cocks her head and reads the pen's logo, ZO. When she takes the pen in her hand she sees that it actually says, ON. As she signs her name it becomes clear that in fact it says, OZ, which makes sense, for they want to build a road, something to get from there to here, here to there. But when she hands back the pen, the logo cries out its true meaning: NO. She looks at the man's folder; it says NO. The logo on his shirt pocket says NO.

But it is too late, she has already signed the paper, he is already slipping it into the file, clicking shut the pen, zipping his black bag, holding out his hand. When her palm meets his she mouths the word, "No," thinking of all the things it rhymes with.

Here does not rhyme with there. Most people are here, trying to get ahead to there, but Maugham is here, and there is somewhere behind her, where she used to be. There is where her girls depended on her for meals and Band-aids and booster seats. Here they depend on her for nothing, as if she is invisible. Maybe she is. She wishes she were there.

She shuts the front door behind the man as he leaves and watches him through the foyer window. She can tell from the profile of his pursed lips, as he jaunts across the sidewalk beyond the landscaping, that he is whistling. And she cannot help but think of an amusement park game target that she should be shooting with some sort of gun.

When they begin digging it registers only as a minor headache, a muffled throbbing, which must mean her brain is moist and scoops easily. But when the large trucks move backward, the beeps bounce around like a racquetball in a hollow court. How much space could there be in her head?

But Maugham has never been very good with spatial relationships. She hadn't realized her own house was so large until the first time she was alone there. They hadn't the furniture to fill it, and when she answered the telephone her voice bounced from one angled, vaulted wall to the next like a runaway cue ball on a billiards table. While the girls were at school she spent her days buying furniture that turned out to be too small. The stores were so large, larger than her house, but filled with a thousand mini-rooms that connected like jigsaw pieces. Each room, she was told, reflected a different style, whether contemporary or casual or country or metropolitan, but Maugham thought they all basically looked the same.

And she thought the furnishings looked like they'd fit in her house but they didn't. Measuring didn't help. She'd return home and stretch her tape measure across the empty living room floor, but find it impossible to mentally fill in the air space with a slab of stuffed leather. Everything fit wrong; nothing fit. With each purchase her house came to look more and more like a disproportionate diorama. Walls tall like mountainsides. The ceilings: skies.

So it was possible that the space inside her head was much bigger than she imagined.

When Maugham was a child it was the outside world that was large and the inside of the house that was small. Now it was all reversed. Now there was a road in her head.

The man with the tie had told her some of what to expect. He said that when the men uprooted trees and cleared away debris from her skull cavity it would feel oh, you know, like a strand of hair getting yanked out at the root. But the man had obviously not had a strand of hair on his head for quite some time, and when he told her this she stared at the shine of chandelier on the surface of his head. Now she knows the plucking and yanking is much more like that of a tooth being pulled too soon by eager, adult hands.

At night her daughters appear for a meeting of the Not-So-United Nations. Each comes to the kitchen table with preferences about the cuisine and demands regarding peace and war. Usually Maugham tries be an ambassador of agreement, but tonight their floating words burn into fireballs and hang as silent stars. Oh to wish upon them instead of against them.

The eldest daughter turns up the volume of the radio and a voice calls out, "Do it do it do it, baby, don't!" The eldest is dancing.

The youngest is shouting, "Don't! Don't!"

The middle daughter reaches her hand toward the volume dial and the oldest smacks the middle's forearm.

"Get off!" they both say. "Don't!"

Maugham can hardly tell whether they are yelling or laughing, whether it is with or at each other, whether they are fighting or friendly. When she clutches her ears and yells, "Stop it! Turn that off!", the noise of the nations is replaced by inner echoes of construction crews pouring concrete and steamrolling. She closes her eyes: the heat, the heat.

She climbs the stairway to heaven and takes an abundance of headache medicine.

In the background the nations are grumbling: "What's *her* problem?" Maugham asks of the doorknobs, the only sensible objects in the house: "When in the hell is the King of the World going to get home?"

She retreats to the master bedroom, another oversized space, where the whole family could live if it needed to. The room reminds her of the furniture store because it is so large that Maugham had to create several mini-rooms just to divide up the space. There was the reading place, which had no books, but which had a window and a chaise lounge, on which no one ever sat or read; a sleeping place with the king-sized bed that meant she never had to have contact with her husband when she slept; and an entertainment place: an armoire that contained a television instead of clothes because the clothes were in the his and hers closets, which echoed the his and hers sinks, which all seemed to say that the best thing for a family to do was to carry on with separate lives in separate rooms and separate sinks.

But it was also important to create the appearance of family unity, and a final space in the room was devoted to photos arranged in artful clusters between two large, fake fica trees. Although the photos marked many separate periods in the family's history, Maugham could stand before the collage of photos and memory, and lump them all into one significant era, just as all historians do. The Victorian Era, The Byzantine Era, the Depression. These eras covered years, even centuries. Her wall of pictures represented less than two decades, but oh how they captured a singular emotion. The Bygone Era.

You are here. You are not there.

From her bed, where she attempts now to rest her body and head, she can see the gilded rectangles on the distant wall and knows the images by heart. The Good Old Days. Black and whites of all three girls in bathing suits making good use of a blow-up pool and a sprinkler (Maugham sometimes conjures the sounds of the spray of water, the squeals of glee). Studio images of the girls individually and together with pigtails, stuffed sheep props, and a haystack seat (how the photographer had to honk and whistle like a Keystone cop to elicit simultaneous smiles). In each photo a different tooth is missing from each girl. The Lost Era. There are even pictures of Maugham herself, before she was Maugham, placid and unflappable, and her own smiles are real, on the very verge of laughter. In the photos she walks with a birthday cake in her arms, already singing. She squeezes a fleshy toddler in a powder blue princess dress; holds the hand of her kindergartners on all the first days of school. The Mommy Era. If she'd only squeezed harder. Held tighter.

The man from NO returns to say, "We're making good progress. Folks are getting from here to there. It's just that—"

She can tell he wants more, they want more. What rhymes with no?

"—that well, you see—what would you say about a gas station?"

The road has been finished for some time now and Maugham has come to enjoy the smooth, constant vibrations in her head of folks getting from here to there. It feels soothing and tingling at once, like a wooden ball rolling across a back or on the underside of a foot. Here to there, there to here.

Meanwhile, the long-legged nations have grown restless. They are mad at the King of the World, who refuses to let them stay out later on weekends and who scrutinizes the princes of other lands who come to visit, finding none fit. The nations cry out, *Mo-om!*

Maugham is placid, unflappable. Maugham is wise: *Accident has cast them amid strangers in their birthplace, and the leafy lanes they have known from childhood or the populous streets in which they have played, remain but a place of passage.*

The man awaits his answer. The traffic hums through her head.

Once upon a time, Maugham had three little girls. The three little girls smelled like lollipops and diapers. Their hair was as soft and blonde as the top of a white-topped dandelion. When they sat in her lap Maugham absently rubbed their toes, one after the other, like rosary beads. And then one day—or so it now seemed—they were gone. In their place were tall teens with lives of television, texting, tampons. Maugham could never shake the feeling that her three little girls had been taken from her, abducted. And she couldn't help it: she blamed her daughters' teenage selves for taking from her their small selves.

"Before you answer," says the man whose tie is a different color than last time, she thinks, maybe. "Just take a look at the offer. Some pretty good terms if you ask me."

Maugham blinks hard to refocus. She examines the offer, the terms. "Oh," she says, because it rhymes with no.

"If you think about it, a gas station just ensures they get from here to there." The man adjusts his weight and leans closer to her.

Maugham glances at the corner of the table to make sure its hard angle is still between her and the man. His fingers clutching the table's edge are hotdogs that have been in the microwave too long. His eyes are the devil's eggs.

"I mean what if someone ran out of gas on the way?" he says. "Then what?"

Her wits grow sharp. She thinks about it, about what would happen if someone ran out of gas on the way, and marvels that she had not thought of it before. They would be stuck in her head. They'd have to walk miles and they might pass out, see mirages, go insane, drink their own piss, die. She looks up at the hundreds of X's of light that glitter on her ceiling. You are here. Sign here.

She will have no one die in her head. The very prospect is enough to make her say the opposite of no.

He returns a few light-months later to say, "They're wondering about some restaurants. You can't expect to get from here to there without a little something in your tummy!" He pats his tummy, which thumps even louder and lower than Maugham would have expected.

She says she doesn't suppose you can.

She doesn't say that she has given them names, the commuters in her head. Not real names, but Candle, Rim, Locomotif. These are names that would have made her young daughters both puzzled and delighted. "You're silly, Mommy," they'd say. "Then what happened?" And Maugham would tell them an extraordinary story about Candle the Star Lighter who fell in love with Rim the Bee Maker who was deathly allergic to bees. She'd always felt like a magician the way she could make her daughters' faces open wide with surprise, shrink with doubt, pinch with concern, grow still with fear, and poof into relief with a happy ending. The Story Era.

The man must feel the need to reassure Maugham because he says, "Nothing fancy, of course. You want to start with the franchises—tried-and-true, red-white-and-blue."

But Maugham needs little convincing. She's not sure when or how the stories started, but now they unfold in her mind with the regularity of a soap opera, and she tunes in every day. Candle and Rim—the whimsical names take her back, back to there—they pass each other on the road twice each day. Candle is the first to notice that the same Studebaker grill appears, heading toward her, at nearly the same spot each morning, and at the same—but different—spot each evening. Candle seeks the face of the driver behind the windshield glass, and in those briefest of moments when the two pass, Candle discerns tension in the morning face, and emptiness in the evening. Candle herself feels tense in the mornings, empty in the evenings, and it is only when she sees her own feelings reflected back to her in the mirror of this other person's face that she feels something else, something she feared she was no longer capable of feeling. These fleeting moments, morning and evening, are the two poles that hold up the droopy telephone wire of her day.

Rim is tense indeed as he drives to work. "You are dying," his doctor had said. "You have, perhaps, two years." Had it been two months, Rim might do something outrageous. Two years, Rim thinks, is not an amount of time one can hold in one's hand. It's like being asked to hold an airplane, one that cannot fly. And outrageous has never appealed to him. So he drives to work every morning, like always, wondering why he continues to do so, what else he might do with his remaining time instead. And each night, having come up with nothing, he returns home, spent.

Locomotif is a mystery, even to Maugham. Locomotif wears circles and circles of cheap metal jewelry on her wrists, upper arms, and neck, like medieval armor. Raccoon eyeliner. Her rusty compact car is part school locker, part trash bin. A cassette tape is stuck in the player, so the only available music is side two of The Doors Greatest Hits. Rewind, replay. But every day at 3:00 Locomotif drives in one direction, and at 5:00 drives the other direction, like a train. Where does she go, Maugham wonders. It's too short for a job shift. Too unlikely that this girl would participate in an organized intermural activity. Maugham can see everything but the here and the there.

"Yes," Maugham says, agreeing with the man. These people of hers need food. A place to stop and rest so she can get to know them better.

She only feigns resistance before signing beside the X.

The man leaves and later Maugham hears the sound of her house's garage door opening, and the indistinguishable voices of the girls and some number of their friends arriving from some sort of athletic practice. They travel in a pack of ponytails to the basement, where even more space is carved out. For the house is more than just expansive rooms, skylighted ceilings, and bulging bay windows. Even the space underground has been dug out, drywalled, and decorated, like previously unknown territory in a southern hemisphere that is now colonized and civilized.

Upstairs, she can't hear the girls and Maugham can convince herself that she is the only person in the house. And when that thought alarms her, after an entire day of being alone (minus a visit from the man from NO), she has to work even harder to convince herself she is *not* alone.

Sure enough, Locomotif is among the first customers at Tacobel, where she orders a Totem Burrito and a Carbo-Pop, and writes with a plastic Bic pen in a speckled Composition notebook, where Maugham can, if she closes her eyes and concentrates, discern some of the contents. There is not much writing, mostly drawings, in blue ink with the pen pressed firmly through multiple pages. Drawings of mythological and religious symbols, dragon heads and other images that usually get etched onto the skin as tattoos. At Tacobel, Locomotif sketches a beautiful woman with long hair and high cheekbones, standing like a superhero. Now she puts lines through that same face, and wrinkles and circles around the eyes. She overlays the figure with a shrunken posture and withering limbs, streaks in the hair that conjure gray. Thou Shalt Not Die, she writes at the top of the page. Please, she adds in cursive at the bottom. Then she puts her pen to the final *e* of Please, and stretches it into a new, looping shape. She does the same with the *P* and the *l* until the word disappears and the word becomes nothing but a whirlpool on the edge of a larger rippling lake under the woman's feet. Locomotif looks at one of the three watches on her wrist, gathers her things, takes her tray full of wrappers to the trash, and heads toward wherever it is she goes every day at 3:00.

Locomotif can't be much older than Maugham's eldest, and Maugham is tempted more than once to tell her daughter the story. But her daughter is surrounded by other stories, stories of teachers and friends with names as unlikely as the ones Maugham has come up with for her commuters. Her daughter returns from school, drops her backpack on the floor like a load of rocks, zips and unzips zippered compartments, and rails about her Math teacher, her Social Studies teacher, her Gym teacher ("the perv"), and refers to the names of at least a half-dozen of the pigtailed friends Maugham has seen walking from the laundry room to the basement, but whom she couldn't identify in a pre-game line-up. When did Maugham stop knowing who her daughters' friends were? Not to mention their teachers!

In the kitchen Maugham eavesdrops, pretending to look for the can opener, while her daughters compare notes on the day ("Another day in paradise"), exchange advice ("All you have to do is ask Mr. Stewart about his stupid dog and he'll shut up about the Civil War or whatever"), and gossip, at which point their voices get low. *Do it do it do it, baby, don't.*

"Found it!" Maugham calls out, holding up the can opener. In pretending to look for it, she found that did not in fact know where it was. Her daughters stare at her as if to say, or perhaps they do say (there is a sudden noise her head), "And your point is?"

Not: "You're silly, Mommy. Then what happened?"

The noise is a car pulling into a parking lot, a car door opening and shutting. It's Candle. She's on her way home, and she stops for a decaf coffee, but when the waitress arrives, Candle forgets or neglects to say decaf, and she is three refills into her bottomless cup of caffeine when, on the other side of the window, she sees a familiar Studebaker grill with glowing lights heading directly toward her table. Will it drive through the window and crash into her table? Is that what makes her body pulse with electrical currents, the sudden knowledge that the car she observed twice every day was her own personal wingéd chariot?

Above or through the reflection of his headlights, Rim sees a head with eyes like stars and a look of what can only be love, and in that moment he knows exactly what he will do with the rest of his short life.

Maugham's back is to her daughters, her eyes are filled with tears.

What was once an open commute now requires—the man from NO has returned to explain—additional lanes, increased signage, a few adjustments to the drainage system.

Yes, Maugham says, reaching for the pen. Yes to all that. Yes to more restaurants and gas stations. Yes to traffic lights, parking lots, strip malls. These things are like an obstacle course that keeps Locomotif, Candle, Rim, and others in the space of her head—somewhere between here and there— slowing them down, surrounding them with instant food, and luring them to linger over caffeinated coffee. She signs here and here and here.

Eventually, though, the concrete begins to crack, car tires slam into potholes. Maugham can feel each thump like a muscle-man's sledgehammer at the county fair. There have been a few fender benders, and now she lives in fear of something worse. Her fear is not for herself, not, any longer, of having someone die in her head. She is concerned now about the people, their well-being.

Whether she is folding laundry, or at the grocery store purchasing colorful food products she doesn't like to eat, or, as she is now, watching one of her daughters perform one of their sports in an echoey gym, she is unable to concentrate on what is there, in front of her eyes. Her attention is on what is happening within, behind her eyes.

"Go Blue!" the other parents yell, as if with a megaphone directly into Maugham's ear. "Defense!"

A child calls, "Mo-om!" Maugham is placid (it is not her child), Maugham is unflappable: *They may spend their whole lives among their kindred and remain aloof among the only scenes they have ever known.*

A very loud buzzer goes off. Numbers change on the scoreboard. A sudden friction of tires skidding in her head snags Maugham's attention; the smash of a collision makes her wince in pain—and worry. She clutches her head. Locomotif? Candle?

A whistle blows. In front of her, one of Maugham's daughters is leveraging her body to receive or intercept a ball; the other parents are calling her name, praising her: "That's it! You got it!"

Inside her, someone is hurt. She hadn't expected to feel like this about the people in her head, but she has come to rely upon their constant companionship, their easy ways. Locomotif's daily journeys, Maugham has learned, are to visit her dying grandmother. Candle and Rim are beginning the end of Rim's life together.

No matter how her own daughters succeed, Maugham feels they have failed her. They don't need her. These talented, beautiful, accomplished girls—for they are all of those things—are the thieves of their younger selves, of those tiny beings who were so very demanding of food and affection and Maugham's stories, so very generous with laughter and play. Maugham had them—their bodies that gave and stretched like Silly Putty—for too short of a time.

And, yes, of course, Maugham has failed her daughters too. She doesn't know their teachers' names, for god's sake. Not to mention their friends'. She is raising them in an oversized house where she herself is not at home. All borders and passports, a tower of Babel. *Do it do it do it, baby, don't.*

"Mo-om!" A voice calls out amid all the other noise. Maugham looks hopefully at her own daughter, who is, of course, not calling for Maugham, who is yelling to someone else, "Pass it!"

Perhaps it is this sense of strangeness that sends men far and wide in the search for something permanent, to which they may attach themselves.

All at once the adults on the bleachers stand up and yell. The younger siblings look up from their games of Skittle-checkers to see what the excitement is about. The oversized gym makes Maugham think of her dining room, where she signed beside so many X's, a whole constellation. You are here. But where? In front of her is a sporting match. Inside her is an accident. She needs to get help for the people in the accident. Candle? Rim? They need her; they are her people. Her daughter doesn't need her, not this one, not the others. (Right?) Another buzzer sound rips through the room, and the crowd is clapping and stomping its feet. She has to get to NO.

Outside the gym, the night is remarkably calm. No steel-rimmed fluorescent lights, no one yelling or clapping, no exploding buzzers, no raw echoes—just flat land, tall trees, and silent starlight. It makes one want to stop and breathe. The rows and rows of minivans are like a herd of grazing buffalo. Their illuminated tops glow in the starlight like lines of shining swords. In another life Maugham might have pointed to the sliver of light on her own car and said, "Look, see the sword? This is our secret weapon against everything bad." And her daughters would nod in earnest agreement, knowing they were safe. They had a mother who knew how to protect them. They had a sword made of light.

Now Maugham recalls her task and hurries to find her own minivan, which alights and chirps like an obedient mechanical toy when she pushes the button on her key chain. She steers herself through the parking lot like a mouse in a maze, and finds herself on the road toward NO.

Sometimes a man hits upon a place to which he mysteriously feels that he belongs. Here is the home he sought, and he will settle amid scenes that he has never seen before, among men he has never known, as though they were familiar to him from his birth. Here at last he finds rest.

There is more traffic on the road than Maugham expected, and she is stopped at one red light, then another. She resumes her speed and passes a row of fast-food restaurants, realizing she is hungry, even for this food. Maybe it will help her headache? No, no, she will not stop, she must get help for the people in the accident. Candle? Rim! She is on her way. They need her. They are the only ones who need her anymore. She will not stop, not even when the approaching car in the center lane turns, too soon, in front of her. Maugham swerves to the left and slams her foot on the brakes to avoid hitting another car in the opposite lane, where she now finds herself. It is here, in the opposite lane, with her head throbbing and a car approaching in an unavoidable way, that she thinks, quite lucidly, as if she had all the time in the world, rather than a millisecond, to ponder it: maybe her daughters do need her. And: what a silly thought. Of course they do. And: it's certainly not too late to learn their teachers' names. But it is too late because the car is coming, coming, too fast to—

Beyond the night clouds, beyond even the stars, a woman winces in pain. She knows that someone has been hurt inside her head; there was skidding, the crush of contact. This woman's son is on the stage, playing second violin, an instrument she calls an irritant, for the god-awful sounds it makes in the house. But here it is muffled by the sounds of two dozen other partially out-of-tune instruments doing a general disservice to Beethoven. She pretends to read the program and only claps because everyone else does. But, oh dear! Her head. She drops the program at her feet. There has been an accident. Is it Maugham? She must find help. It's urgent. These are her people. She rises from her seat, goes out to the parking lot, gets in her car, and starts the engine.

FOR SALE BY OWNER

The white duplex on the corner lot, which, when I first noticed the For Sale By Owner sign in the narrow path between the street and the sidewalk, had appeared slouched and even, I suppose, insolent, now looked (as I eyed it suspiciously from my spot in the passenger seat) as if it had sucked in its breath and was standing at ready—and nearly ready to fall out of—attention. I thought of a dog at the pound, a child at an orphanage, trying to be picked.

"I think he trimmed the bushes," my husband said as he turned off the ignition.

My hand pressed down on my belly. "The baby's moving," I said.

We climbed up the front porch, which was splintered and peeling, and, as we had been instructed, rang the bell of the door on the right. As the door opened, something made me reach—uncharacteristically—for my husband's hand. And when, a moment later, Frank released my grip to shake hands with the man at the door, my palm felt as empty and exposed as if I had just dropped a stack of dishes. If I had been able to tell Frank how I felt, he would have said I was being dramatic, that my hormones were getting the best of me, and I would have had to agree (even if I did not).

The man at the door must have been exactly sixty. Mr. Rogers comes to mind as someone who was exactly sixty for the entire thirty years he was on television. The man at the door was like a negative—or perhaps a positive—of Mr. Rogers. He was tall and lean, and he wore a cardigan sweater, but his sweater was yellow and his pants and shoes were white. Even his gray hair was combed over to one side and touched with blond, so he also reminded me of Pat Boone, another person who could only and always have been sixty.

In a welcoming gesture, he raised his hand and turned his palm toward his face but left it there—the three of us looking up at it—a moment too long. "Come in, come in," he said, finally, nervously, and turned his back to us.

As Frank and I stepped inside and the man faced us again, I breathed in the strong and familiar scent of Vitalis, the same hairspray my grandfather used, and I relaxed—though I was not sure why I was not relaxed—a little.

"This here, of course," he said, mixing the accent of the slightly uneducated Midwesterner with a touch of southern gentility, "is the entry, or the foy-ay, as it were."

We were standing on a clear, plastic carpet-protector, which split in the middle of the foyer, forming a large Y, and led to two different doorways. We turned our heads up and to the sides and nodded. There was not much to see. Beige wall-to-wall carpet covered the floor, and the walls were white, with a tan trim along the baseboards and around the windows. At least, I thought, we wouldn't have to worry about tearing down layers of wallpaper. The entry opened up into what had probably been a dining area, but in which there was only a small table with a rotary telephone beside the right arm of the plastic Y.

Frank stepped back as the man reached over to open a closet door. "Some nice closet space," the man muttered, and it was (nice, that is), but it was empty. It was under the steps leading up to the other apartment, and queer, jagged shadows fell across the various surface planes, and as I peered into its darkness I thought, for some reason—perhaps because of my hormones, or perhaps because of the preposterous nature of an empty closet, or perhaps because my father drowned himself when I was six and so I often think of this—of all the things that must lie at the bottom of the river.

The man closed the door and stepped past me to take a position at the edge of what he called the living room. He extended his arm and seemed to puff out his chest like one of Hemingway's bullfighters. A clean, off-white sofa stood alone against the left wall and faced the front windows from which hung long, creamy drapes. The carpet had tracks from a vacuum, but they didn't seem like fresh tracks: they might have been there, un-walked on, for months. I felt, upon looking at all the white and off-white, as if I were staring into a light bulb that was burning itself into my eyes. I looked down at the navy blue of my protruding belly for relief, and I felt the little life stir inside me.

I suppose I should say at this point (though perhaps I should have said it already?) that Frank and I were not of one mind about our next home. Married almost two years, we were renting a one-bedroom apartment that was already beginning to fill up with large boxes of baby gear: a stroller, car seat, swing, exersaucer, and port-a-crib were grouped and stacked in a corner, obstructing access to a closet door as well as to a small bookshelf, like oversized cinder blocks. We hadn't opened the boxes because we were hoping to move before the baby was born, though we were running out of time. I wanted to buy a single-family home and create a magical, protected world for my baby boy (I hadn't told Frank, who wanted our first child to be a surprise, but I knew it was a boy). Frank, always more practical—except when it came to learning the sex of his firstborn—and ready for a challenge, thought it would be smart (Frank was never stupid) to buy a two-family home and offset some of the mortgage by renting out a unit. We could buy a more expensive property than if we bought a single family, and with the rent money along with what we would save in childcare, I would be able to quit my job.

I used to spend my days cutting (and cutting, and cutting) hair. You should see how much I would sweep up at the end of a day. I often thought to scoop up a handful and, like the Sibyl with her sand, ask to live as many years. (And I even imagined I would not later ask to die.) I would mix hair color like I once mixed paints in college. I'd dab my brush and apply the color in a smooth stroke down a section of hair. But the canvas was so blissfully silent—allowing *me* to speak through it, of rivers and currents, coursing like blood, like a disease—and the clients were so full of words and stories, always talking and talking as I was cutting and cutting. I would come home with so many parts of stories attached to me, I'd feel like Frankenstein's monster. I would try to tell this to Frank, but he wanted to know only whether my clients tipped as well as they talked.

Reader, may I be frank? I wish to speak frankly of my marriage. I married Frank because the first time I saw him, he was bent over tying his shoe, like my father was on the last morning before he floated away from me. It was my first year of cutting hair after years of painting rivers, and I was old enough to marry this image of my father and, I imagined, to stop what my mother couldn't. No, that is not why I married Frank. That is why I noticed Frank. I married Frank because he turned out to be nothing like my father after all. My mother only spoke of my father in vague terms of absence: he was "not here," he was "gone," we were "without" him. Because I don't know the grown-up reasons for why he did it and because his absence has always been such an overwhelming presence, I created a story about my father from the dawn of my memory. It is a romance: Once upon a time my father was in love with Life. He courted her and kissed her and made music for her. When he was old enough, he married her. Together they laughed and made more life (me). They lived together happily, happily, until Life's Enemy seduced my father with promises of more. She convinced him that what he had was not enough, that some treasure awaited him at the bottom of the water. And one day, one cruel spring day, he tied his shoes and dove for the treasure and did not return. Without him, Life was silent and sad.

But I was speaking frankly of my marriage. The good thing is that I do not have to worry about Frank killing himself.

The man led us to his bedroom, which contained a double bed, a desk with a neat stack of *TV Guides* along with what I would later learn were racing forms, a television on a cart, and a dresser with a large mirror above it. On the nightstand were two remote controls and, to my surprise, a sign of life: a photograph. In it, the man, looking about ten years younger, stood with a group of people surrounding a dark horse and a jockey. One person was holding up a large gold plate, there were roses strung around the neck of the horse, and everyone was smiling broadly. They were all looking at the camera, except for the man, whose eyes were focused on the gold plate. I knew the racetrack; it was a few miles south, on the banks of the river.

"I bet you won some money on that horse," I said teasingly, though I was not at ease, not at all.

He looked at me, then at the picture. He drew his middle finger across a stray hair on his forehead and said, *"Heiress* was her name."

And then we were crowded in the white, of course white, bathroom where there was a Dixie cup dispenser and a hand towel. My blood felt thin, and I became light-headed. I wondered which porcelain surface I would hit when I fell. Would I bleed—red, like the roses on the horse, like a bullfighter's cape—against the whiteness? Everything was so clean, so clean and white. I asked for some water and leaned against the wall. Frank checked the water pressure and the pipes. There were feminine pads under the sink.

"Those belong to my lady friend." The man must have seen me staring at them, unable, in this sixty-year-old's bachelor pad, in my dizzy state, to figure out what they were doing there.

A lady friend. I nodded, feeling better. Blood absorption.

And then we were climbing stairs, the stairs above the empty foyer closet, and I was feeling the weight of the extra thirty pounds I was carrying—thinking about the twenty-five pounds of blood and fluid (the blood I did not bleed for eight months), flowing like a river that I sometimes feared would drown the five pounds of baby. The man was saying that he had grown up in this house, in the apartment we were about to see. That his family had been the first and only owners of the house. That there was no one left in the family. That he wanted (or had he said needed?) to pass it on.

The upstairs apartment, he told us, was being rented by a woman and her teenage son. The antithesis of the downstairs dwelling, it was littered with clothes, bills, video games and CDs, the remains of snacks, and if I had not felt as though I'd just been transported from a stark and barren arctic to a lush and warm, if somewhat chaotic, rainforest, I would have been appalled. Instead I was drawn to it, to wanting to fix it up—the way one is drawn to donate the cost of a cup of coffee to a child on television.

"He's a real good boy," the man said of the woman's son. "He trimmed the hedges this week, and he works on his mom's car, trying to fix it up. This is his room." We were standing in the doorway of a room at the front of the house. "It used to be mine growing up," he said. "But see, my bed was over there against that wall, and over here," he pointed, "over here's where I kept my toy soldiers. I had a whole collection of them." He paused, blinked his eyes, and looked back at us. "I'll show you the bathroom."

I realized I had been rubbing my belly and my fingers felt hot and tingly. I lingered a moment at the door, thinking the room—once the scratched-up guitar and amp, the rock posters, the smelly clothes were gone—would make a great nursery. I envisioned the crib with a slow-turning mobile and fresh paint. I would paint again. No more rivers. Yellow and blue: stars and sky for my baby boy.

"I had to replace the old bathtub," I heard the man explain to Frank as I approached the bathroom. "It was cracked and had those old claw feet, you see, and I put in this new one with a shower head."

As he had done before, Frank turned the faucets on full power in the sink and tub, then flushed the toilet to check the water pressure.

"And this room," he said, leading us into the adjacent sunroom, "is where my uncle stayed when he lived with us for a couple of years—well, more than a couple—after his wife died. He kept a chair right in front of that window and stared down at what was the top of that oak tree there. Now the tree's taller than the house."

As Frank asked questions—*was the structure sound, had the tree roots caused any shifting in the foundation, were there problems with flooding, with insects, with rodents*—I pictured myself sitting in the sunroom on a rocking chair nursing my baby. I would paint the walls, maybe lavender, and put plants all around. I would sing and smile and coo.

And so went the rest of the tour of the second floor: The old man sidestepping the piles of messes on the floor and leading us around like a docent, telling stories. Frank checking the water pressure and asking questions about furnaces and fuel efficiency which neither I nor, I presumed, the old man cared much about. And I imagining the new paint, the decorations, the baby sleeping. None of us was paying attention to the others. Reader, are you paying attention? Someone needs to be paying attention.

The third floor was one long room; the ceiling slanted down on both sides, like a tunnel running from the front to the back of the house. It was an unfinished addition to the second-floor apartment, and there was an old couch and TV, a stained carpet remnant, and an ashtray on the floor. The man walked around the carpet and across the bare wood floor to the back window. He smoothed his hair over with his hand and bent to look out at the rows of rooftops.

"I used to climb out this window and just sit on the roof for hours all by myself. I didn't have any siblings. My mother delivered two dead babies after me. None of those houses out there were even here yet, you see. This was all just land, and from up here on this roof I thought I could see the whole world. And for all I know, I could. I never traveled much beyond what you can see from this roof."

We three stood together, silent at last, staring out the back window at the angles and planes of rooftops and telephone wires and treetops under an almost unbearably heavy gray sky. I wished he hadn't said "dead babies."

"Well," he turned to us, "As I say, I'm the only one left in my family, so I reckon it's time see the rest of the world. I thought I'd give Florida a whirl." He seemed to be trying to smile, and so I smiled back to let him know I didn't believe him. Not for a second.

As we followed the man back down the narrow staircase, he said over his shoulder, "I see you've got a little one on the way."

"Just a few more weeks to go," I managed to say, though I did not like him—this man with no furniture who spoke of dead babies—talking about my son. I cradled my stomach protectively.

"I always wondered what that would be like," he said as he opened the door and stepped onto the front porch and breathed in the chilled air, "to have life growing inside of you."

Perhaps he said *a* life, but I don't think so, and it should be, but it is not, too much to say that at that moment I felt as if an opera singer was hitting her highest and loudest note right in my ear.

We bought the house (it seemed, somehow, to want to be free of the man, to be fixed up and made over, and I allied myself with its cause) and moved into the upstairs apartment where Frank spent evenings, weekends, and his week-long paternity leave cleaning, painting (I let him do it after all), hauling things to the trash left behind by the previous tenants, and installing new fixtures. Glad not to have to worry about renting out the downstairs unit right away, we (read: *Frank*) agreed to let the old man stay on a few months until he could get his plans together to leave. He disappeared in his Buick for a couple of hours in the middle of almost every day. I never saw any lady friend.

I was busy now in the way new mothers are busy and not busy, caring for Alexander (he'd made it out of my bloody rivers: he coughed and cried and took in the air) and listening to his stories of "goo" and "gaa." Except for when I heard his car outside, I hardly thought about the man downstairs. And yet whenever I came or went through the door beside his on the front porch, I felt as if I were—and possibly I was—holding my breath. I would draw Alexander closer to my breast (and feel our hearts beat together) with the same impulse that compelled me to grab Frank's hand that first day.

The held breath, whether metaphorical or literal, was released one afternoon. I had been out that morning with Alexander for his three-month check-up, and returned to find an envelope (without a stamp), addressed to the police, jutting out from my mailbox.

The man, we would learn, had been overwhelmed by gambling debts, of the mostly illegal kind, at the racetrack. The money from the sale of the house had not been enough. His lady friend was "friends" with many others at the track. He had never made even a phone call to Florida.

The man had begun—that morning, while we were at the doctor's office getting Alexander his immunizations (do they have one for this?)—by slitting his wrists. But when the blood started running all over his white clothes, his white bathroom (where I had been dizzy—for it is in my blood, and in Alexander's blood), and when he was not dying fast enough, he put a gun (which had been there, just in case) to his forehead and pulled the trigger. The last line of the note was addressed to Frank and me: an apology, in advance, for the mess.

Frank was not there and I will never tell him this, but I will tell you, reader, for that is what you are here for (you are still here, no?): that, shaking, nearly hyperventilating, I dropped the note and unlocked the man's door. I went directly to the bathroom. I stood at the door and held my son before the frozen, bloody scene, and cried, "Don't you ever, *ever*, do this!"

BIOGRAPHY OF YOUR HUSBAND

Biography of Your Husband takes you deep inside the illicit world of your husband's affairs, bringing them to life in a way your mind has never fully confronted or imagined. Though you have often suspected him of infidelity, this is the first time one of his lovers has made a public claim about a relationship. *But is she telling the truth?* This question looms at the heart of this thorough and compelling biography, which has both the parodic playfulness of Virginia Woolf's *Orlando* and the devoted diligence of Boswell's *Life of Samuel Johnson*. Packed with deep psychological insight and rich dramatic tension, *Biography of Your Husband* provides the mistress's moving account of your husband's motives, of the many times you almost caught him, and of her role in the affair. Smitten, the author, devoted countless research hours into an investigation of your husband's childhood, his dreams, his goals, and his desires, and she offers an unflinchingly honest and hauntingly persuasive, if occasionally naïve, defense of why she believes *she* is the better partner for your husband. Along the way Smitten also details many incidents that other authors (and lovers) would shy away from and that corroborate her claims. In the end, it is up to you to decide if you believe her and if so, what you will do about it.

Praise for *Biography*:
"Dazzling, riveting, revealing...shows your husband in a new light...if this doesn't help you confront your marital problems, nothing will..." – *The New York Times*

"*Biography of Your Husband* made me laugh and cry in turn...a witty evocation of the contrast between the banalities of your marriage and the alternate life your husband may or may not lead." – *Esquire*

"Read this book—if you dare!" – *Entertainment Weekly*

About the Author
Jane Smitten lives and writes at the edges of your consciousness, of your property, peering in the windows of your life after the rest of the neighborhood has gone to bed. You sense her presence in your every

maternal deed and (attempted) romantic encounter—watching, judging. Her smile is the moon's crescent rising over the mountains of her cleavage at twilight. She has been tempting your husband for years, perhaps, but her success is always entirely dependent upon you. You hope. Or do you? She will continue to exist inasmuch as you will let her, though it is possible she will exist regardless. She knows how hard you work to stitch up the bursting seams of your marriage for the children, for stability—and she knows you are almost out of thread. She does not know that you pricked your finger and put it to your lips and that you are now thirsty for blood. She is aware that your husband won't take action—that it is up to you. And she is no longer content to watch and wait. She wants you to know your husband's story. She wants to be seen. Read. Acknowledged. She wants to know if you're ready. She has no idea how ready you are.

THE COMPLETE BABYSITTER'S HANDBOOK

Not Dead

Anne did not die. Even if at the moment she is not so sure. Her brain scrabbles about in her sore head like a mouse in the dark. The lid of her left eye lifts, and her brain races toward the light, surveys the scene (fluorescent bulb, dowdy curtain attached to ceiling: no one's idea of an afterlife), and then retreats behind the exhausted eyelid. Her brain perks to sounds coming from the other side of the curtain—a stranger in pain—then curls up into itself and goes to sleep.

Some time later a female voice with a watered-down southern accent says, "Another inch or so toward the temple might have killed her."

Anne hears these words clearly—no scrabbling mouse this time—and opens her left eye quickly and fully. Her right eye, swollen as it is, does not respond to the signal. There is a woman standing above her, a silhouette surrounded by glaring fluorescent light. God?

"Well, hello," says the figure above her in a different voice than she has just heard. This one is balmy, soothing, as lilting as the words, *well, hello.*

When Anne tries to reply, her words get stuck on something hard and plastic pressing down on her tongue. She tries to smile instead, but pain shoots across her face. She settles on blinking her one good eye.

The first voice speaks again. "The police are questioning her husband in the waiting room right now."

Anne rotates her left eye in its socket in search of the speaker. Just beyond her regular vision, in her peripheral vision, is a stout middle-aged female figure wearing a uniform not unlike the curtain hanging from the ceiling. The woman above her moves from the front of the light and the light burns Anne's eye, which shuts like a trap. When Anne opens her eye again, the woman is writing something on a clipboard. Anne sees her long white jacket, the stethoscope around her neck, and begins to understand: doctor, nurse, hospital. But she does not understand the rest: husband, police, questioning.

The doctor's haircut, Anne notices, is like a pageboy's, though the actual word *pageboy* eludes her at the moment. She is leaning over Anne again, this time with a metal instrument against her own eye, and telling Anne to look up, down, right, left, while she shines a hot beam into her eye.

"Good," the doctor says. "I'll be back after you've had some more rest."

Anne hears polysyllabic words as the two women leave: *intraparenchymal hemorrhage, cerebral swelling.* And she closes her eye. But she does not rest. She tries to remember why she is here. But her memory has been affected not just by whatever happened, but by the way she has recorded her past. What she remembers is not her life so much as the Memory Book pages she has made of it. Even now her mind can access various recollections according to a photographic memory of specific pages, chronological highpoints of happiness. Last Halloween, for example, comes to mind easily. Krissy in her majorette costume (hand-sewn to look like Anne's mother's majorette costume); Jared as Spiderman; Rob drinking a beer that Chuck across the street offered him as a "treat." She did not include in the Memory Book any photos of the fight she and Rob had over him drinking the beer—which turned into several beers—that night, so that part doesn't even come to her mind. Rob, she knows, equals husband. She knows too that she feels a different pain, something deep in her gut, when she thinks of him. But she has no Memory Book of the last month of their lives, no photos framed by colorful borders with carefully planned captions, and she can't remember why she's here.

Into The Belly Of The Dragon

Rob finally does what the police and doctors tell him to do, which is to go home (and not to get any ideas about going anywhere else). He knows enough to be relieved that Anne didn't die, but it's not like he was really trying to *kill* her, for God's sake. If she had died, well, he'd really be pissed at her then, but at the same time, her survival strikes him as another of her little victories. She'll be holding this against him forever and a day.

Rob settles his mind that he will maintain the story he told the neighbors when he imposed the kids on them so many hours ago, even if the kids have gone and blabbed about the fighting. Anne tripped on the table and hit her head—okay, yes, in the middle of a fight, if you must know. The doctors say she'll be fine. Okay? Now can I get my kids?

No, he assures himself, he hadn't tried to kill her. He'd just wanted to hit her out of the park—so to speak—with that long, sleek silver lamp she bought at Target or wherever, her head coming toward him smooth but not steady, like a knuckleball. But he'd struck too high, and wasn't this why he hadn't made it out of the minors to begin with? The fastball would come faster, the curve ball would curve harder, and the slider would fling wider than his brain could ever adjust to. Even though he knew from experience what a pitch could do, it always took him by surprise in the batter's box. If he hadn't been such a good second-baseman and base runner, he wouldn't have made it so far. But, in the end, who cares if you're a good runner if you never get on base. Alas, only pitchers could get away with not being able to.bat.

By God those were good days. He would've been content on the farm team forever: being called The Robber for his ability to steal bases, traveling, drinking, and always, always hoping. But the management turned on him when they figured out he'd never become a batter. And that was that.

Still, it was farther than any of his high school buddies had gone, and that kind of thing made a difference when it was time to find a real job. A couple of his friends had already signed on to Gary Klein's family insurance business and were doing well for themselves—but not so well that they weren't interested in an almost-pro ball-player joining their ranks. No sooner did he get himself a job than he found himself a fiery blonde— hired, unlike himself, on merit rather than nepotism—whose quarterly sales topped those of all the men, and who happened to be the slightest bit weak-kneed in the presence of the almost-pro ball-player.

But Anne knew how to play the office game. Indeed, she'd been playing keep-away from his buddies for a few years by then. So, what was the difference? Being almost-pro? Maybe. But Rob was well aware that it was also a matter of timing. Anne had proven to herself that she was equal to—hell, better than—the men she worked with. She'd made good money. (He was later sad to see her salary go.) She'd made personal sacrifices to do it. And she was just unfulfilled enough to hope there was something else out there. Rob, who was immediately unsatisfied with his boring-ass job and was doubtful anything would ever be as fulfilling as baseball (almost was), picked up on all this. Rob and Anne occupied themselves with some minor flirting, which led to innocent after-work drinks, which led to a secretive against-office-policy romance (that everyone knew about), which led to an open engagement. Wedding. Kids. The rest.

Rob presses the remote garage-door opener attached to his visor. His muscles are involuntarily trembling. There is his house. Like a sleeping dragon—now yawning, opening its mouth wide. Rob drives into the fiery breath, and the mouth swallows him. He stumbles into the belly of the beast and collapses onto the couch. He will get the children in the morning.

A Visit With The Neighbors

Krissy is reading—is trying to read—*The Complete Babysitter's Handbook* at the neighbor's house when she sees the lights of her father's SUV shine briefly against the small, rectangular windows in the Allens' basement and then turn toward the awaiting light in the garage. As if the two lights—car and garage—have been searching for each other all night and finally found each other. Like true love, she thinks. Maybe. Not that she would know.

She's been uneasy all day, not so much because of Mom being in the hospital—though that sure was freaky to hear her scream and then to be rushed out of the house by Dad like that—but because of being stuck here at the Allens' house. She wishes Dad would've just let them stay at home. She's practically babysitting on her own now—she could've taken care of herself and Jared. In their own house with their own food and video games. No problem.

Luckily she was reading when it happened—*what* happened?—and she had her book in her hand when she was taken next door. But even her *Babysitter's Handbook* wouldn't get her any closer to making money with the Allens' little two-month old, Virginia. "How neat that you're reading that, Krissy," Mrs. Allen had said, bouncing Virginia and patting her back. "Maybe in a few years you'll be babysitting Virginia!" A few years. Hmph. Krissy would have to find someone who wasn't quite so brand-new in the mother department.

All day, though, she and Jared have been bumping up against Mrs. Allen and her strictly adhered-to schedule with Virginia while Mr. Allen worked in the yard (despite the ninety-four degree temperature). Krissy and Jared were sent to the basement during Virginia's naptime, and they were glad for the underground cool and for the escape. They could tell Mrs. Allen didn't know how to interact with the giant children, so unlike her precious blob of baby. At dinner, especially, Mrs. Allen struggled to come up with a menu. "So, what do you two *eat*?" As if they were lions or buzzards. Big chunks of raw meat, please.

Krissy throws a pillow at Jared, who has fallen asleep watching Nickelodeon. He had been especially upset about the day's events. He kept saying to Krissy (away from Mrs. Allen's ears), "They were fighting. They were fighting." "So what's new?" Krissy had said to calm him down and to stop him from saying those disturbing words over and over. She knew it was probably true, what Jared meant—that Dad hurt Mom. But what does an eleven-year-old do with such information? Try to keep the nine-year-old from worrying about it.

"Dad's home," she says when she sees the lights. She says it triumphantly, for it is a release. Whatever happened, everything will be okay; they can go home now. But, wait. Krissy can tell by a subtle change in the lighting beyond the reflection in the window that the timed garage light has just blinked off and that their house is completely dark. That Dad must be inside. That they are sleeping at the Allens' house tonight.

Surely they would've been told if something was really wrong with Mom. But wouldn't they have been told too if everything was fine? No news—Krissy comforts herself with aphorism—is good news.

Jared pulls himself up so he's almost sitting. His long bangs hang across his face and he yawns. "Cool," he says as he comes out of the yawn. "My neck hurts."

"Forget it," she says, feeling—again today—the burden of being a big sister. "Go back to sleep. It was somebody else's car."

Attempted Murder, Part 1

Anne has been awakened again by the throbbing in her head, just behind her right eye, and she lies in the darkened hospital room, remembering how she got there. It comes back to her in ugly images, like in an amateur's Memory Book: strange charges on the credit card bill, a lowered voice on telephone calls, absences unaccounted for by the company. She could've cared less about whatever little Jackie or Jenny that Rob had found to amuse himself, but she guarded jealously the structure of her family unit, the integrity of their Memories.

Anne had come to domestic life differently than many women she knew. She hadn't left the work world prematurely, she hadn't avoided it altogether, and she hadn't tried to do it while raising kids. She just did it. She got in there, beat the pants off of all the men whose eyes were on her ass instead of their paperwork, then she left at the top of her game. No regrets. She was ready for the new challenge of being married and raising a family. Which was not quite what she'd hoped. Quite a bit of stress what with the crying and sleep-loss and the general disappointment. Krissy was too soft and introverted for the plans Anne had for her. Jared such the boy. Never can tell what's going on between those headphones or behind that hair of his. And, before the kids had started kindergarten and the three of them were home together, the days were not always entirely stimulating.

Which is why she started making Memory Books. With the right tools—colorful paper (acid-free), pre-cut borders, stencils, stickers, specialty scissors, spray adhesive, and the right choice of photos—the life she had just lived was transformed into something organized, dynamic, and happy. Like that.

Then, savvy business-woman that she was, she turned her hobby into an extra income. "*Just Book It!*" became her dual-meaning slogan referring to the production of Memory Books as well as to the parties she "booked" to share her ideas and wares with a far-reaching network of creatively-crippled women who welcomed the idea of making their lives (appear) happier.

About a month ago she confronted Rob about his possible affair simply to encourage him to be more careful, lest his dalliances shift the tenuous balance of their union. But what she discovered was that the balance had already been shifted: he'd fallen for his little Suzie or Sally. Sorry, dear, no room for you in the Memory Books.

Which was her basic message to Rob yesterday, for she'd had enough of his carelessness, his smug happiness, his utter disregard. Who do you think you are, etc., she said, and was just warming up when Rob snapped, turned rabid. She hadn't expected it. It was exhilarating. Rob's mouth foamed with rage. Over nothing but a Tammy or Tina! Then—Anne can see it now, even as her left eye stares as the darkened hospital ceiling—there was the lamp with Rob's hands wrung around its neck as if it were a chicken in its last moments. The shade was cocked; the solid, silver base coming at her right eye.

She vaguely recalls the police officer who came to her room earlier. Wanting to know if she wished to press charges against her husband. But at the time she couldn't remember what had happened. All she knew was that there was an ugly picture of her in a hospital bed that needed a caption. The police officer gave her one: Attempted Murder.

Rob Is Greeted With Hugs

Rob awakens, and his first desire is to get the kids. Overnight, the story he will tell has crystallized in his mind, nearly replacing the memory of what actually happened. They were fighting—yes, he will concede that—and in the blindness of their anger she stumbled, tripping on a table leg, and fell against the end table, knocking over the lamp (which should probably figure in, even in this version). There it is now: the lamp on the floor, right where she knocked it over.

He needs the kids around to reassure him that his life has not changed that dramatically—even though he knows it has, or is about to. A change that he has been willing to happen for months, but has put-off for fear that it would be irrevocable. He needs the kids, too, because he feels guilty and sorry and they are the ones for whom he wants to make it all up.

He does *not* want to call Zoey who has been too demanding recently—even with all he's done—and who anyway he sort of blames right now. For a while Zoey was like his Princess Leah, but lately she and Anne, who don't even know each other (for all they know *of* each other), seem to be conspiring against him, coming at him from both sides just like the walls in the *Star Wars* garbage compactor scene. He'd lashed out at one of the sides the day before, and now Anne is in the hospital, and he can only wonder: Now what?

He had wanted Zoey nearer. God, how he'd wanted her nearer. Her soft (red!) hair, lavender-scented skin. Those adorable giggles just before.... Well. She was planning to be nearer soon. Not five hours, but five minutes away in an apartment he agreed to pay for, for her and her (not his) daughter. Now—assuming he can convince them of the accidental nature of Anne's injuries—he could probably have Zoey. Get the divorce, go live in her (messy) apartment. But now he isn't so sure that's what he wants. He wants his own kids. He goes upstairs and changes out of the clothes the Allens saw him in yesterday.

The kids, God love 'em, are as relieved to see him as he is to see them. One on each side clutching his waist, acting as a shield against any inquisitiveness on Liz Allen's part. *Thanks for your help, Liz. My, isn't Virginia getting big? Yes, yes, Anne will be fine. We'll have to plan that barbecue sometime soon, summer's almost over! Okay, thanks again. Bye now.*

When he enters his house now in the brighter light of the morning with his children in tow, it is not nearly so oppressive. It is clean—except for the lamp Anne knocked on the floor—and rather cheerful. Anne has done a nice job with the family photos on the wall. A good-looking family. Yes, he thinks, I like it here.

"Run up and get changed, you two," he says, patting the kids' backs. "We're going to see Mom."

A Ride In A Police Car

Krissy stares at her mother. Her eye is swollen shut. The color of her face is wrong. All those machines. Krissy has always wished she were as pretty as her mother, but now she doesn't look very pretty. She looks terrible, and Krissy wants to run from the room. Although her mother reaches out her hand, Krissy doesn't dare touch her. She looks at her father. Could he have possibly done this? No, she thinks. Maybe. She thinks of something else.

She thinks of her babysitting service. She wants to start her own business just like her mom started a Memory Book business. It's so cool how her mom has that whole room at home full of Memory Book stuff, all organized in containers. How she's got all the records of the money she's made stored in the computer. Krissy isn't really interested in the Memory Books themselves, though they are nice enough, but she loves that her mom has got her own business. Recently, when Krissy said she wanted to have her own company someday too, her mother had kind of laughed in a way Krissy didn't know how to interpret, and chucked her lightly on the chin, saying, "Well, my dear, you're going to have to get a little tougher before that happens."

So, Krissy had been working on getting tougher. She thinks she was pretty tough all day yesterday at the Allens, and she feels pretty tough standing in her mom's hospital room. Though she also feels like she might faint.

Jared is sort of whimpering on Mom's chest, and Mom is petting his hair with an I.V. taped around her wrist. Dad is standing by the door. No one speaks.

Then there is the commotion of doctors and police officers. The doctors want to see her mother—the police officers, her father. Krissy and Jared are ushered out of the room, and then their father is gone and an officer is telling her and Jared that he needs to talk to their daddy down at the station. "It'll be okay," her dad says before he leaves with the officer.

Krissy and Jared sit in the waiting room. Jared listens to his headphones and she reads her book; she wonders what they're waiting for.

At least she likes her book. Chapter Four suggests wearing comfortable clothing that you can get dirty, in case of a baby spitting up, a toddler spilling, or an older child wanting you to play. Krissy, who is very thorough and appreciates this quality in others, is pleased with this tip and puts a star by it even though she doesn't own any other type of clothing than that described.

She hears the squeaking of the police officer's shoes before she sees him. He tells them he is going to take them back home and they'll be staying with their neighbor for a few days, "until Mommy is better." Both children shake their heads in silence when the officer asks them if they know anything about what happened. Did they see anything? Hear anything? Do their parents fight often? Shake. Shake. Shake.

Jared gets to sit in the front of the car where all the controls are, while Krissy sits in the back seat where there are metal bars, rips in the vinyl, and, she is sure, lots of germs.

Attempted Murder, Part 2

Attempted Murder. Anne can actually see the words as if on the Memory Book page: each letter a separate (blood) red sticker mounted individually on one-inch black squares then double-mounted on one-and-a-half-inch white squares, neatly spray-mounted against a (blood) red background. Or better, she can use her computer program to create a faux-newspaper, like she did for Jared's baseball championship, and make it a headline: Attempted Murder. Then there would be room for a full description of the events leading up to the crime (written by the AP, Anne Press) as well as room for a photo of Anne in her hospital bed. She wishes someone would take her picture.

But after her second night in the hospital, she is told she will be released because the insurance company will not cover further in-patient treatment.

"That's it?" Anne—who is able to speak since the tube was removed from her mouth before the kids arrived yesterday—asks the nurse, feeling slighted.

"That's what they tell me," says the nurse, who has just reported to duty and is meeting Anne for the first time.

"But I almost *died*," Anne tells her.

The nurse looks at Anne. "I don't think so," she says.

"My husband," Anne says, finding her matter-of-fact business voice, "almost killed me." She finds she enjoys saying it.

"Hon," says the nurse, who Anne is not sure is younger or older than herself, "just because he almost killed you doesn't mean you almost died. You've got a cerebral contusion—a bruise."

Hmph.

Anniversary Celebration

Rob had gone out of his way to meet Zoey. He'd heard her voice purring on the other end of the phone so many times when he called the Cleveland branch about whatever work he was doing up there, he decided he had to come up with a reason to see her in person. He bought a handful of tickets to an upcoming inter-league Reds and Indians game, and planned to show up at her desk to deliver them to a couple of his buddies up there. "Tell them it's a little something from the Cincy guys," he would (and later did) say. He knew that if (when) his own office heard about the purchase, not to mention the personal delivery, it would cause all sorts of commotion. But it just might be worth it. For it wasn't just the purring quality of Zoey's voice that attracted him. Their business exchanges bordered on innuendo. The slightest, only-noticeable-if-you're-looking pause between "When can you get it up for me?" and "Tomorrow."

So different from exchanges at home: "I thought you were going to get home a half-hour ago." "How could you let the kids *watch* (or *eat* or *do*: insert verb of choice) that?" Most recently: "Do you really think you're going to wear *that* shirt for the pictures?" Ah yes, Anne had been making memories again. This time even more orchestrated than others. They were all going to a park—with a creek, woods, and overlook for optional backgrounds— to get family photos taken. It was almost as bad as trips she arranged to King's Island that he sensed were planned for the sole purpose of having a family picture taken in front of the imitation Eiffel Tower. But at least there they could ride some roller coasters after the photos. This time, they were just putting on a bunch of matching clothes (he'd missed the memo on that one) to stand like statues wherever Anne and the photographer decided, and to curve their lips up as practiced before-hand in the mirror.

In fact, Rob had been getting more and more freaked out by Anne's picture books. Last October she'd insisted that they plan a "romantic" evening for their anniversary. He hardly knew what she was talking about. But sure, a nice dinner, some sort of live performance, fine. She planned it all, of course, and when she told him the name of the restaurant and that it would be not some boring old orchestra or opera but a Lyle Lovett show, Rob got pretty excited. About the itinerary, but even, by association, about Anne. He'd forgotten how damned cute her nose was there at the end where it turned up, how pretty and even her teeth were, how round those breasts. He'd actually called her "Sweets" a few times as the date approached. Anne had seemed pleased but distracted in her usual way.

The night arrived, and Anne looked really stunning in what must've been a new black dress that spread across her neck in a wide V that left her shoulders and neck bare but for an elegant, sparkly necklace that he suddenly wished he'd bought for her. Her figure had stretched out a bit over the years, but the black dress hugged her curves beautifully, revealed every one, and he found himself forgetting how cold and mechanical their relationship had grown as he surveyed this flesh-and-blood being that he'd married thirteen years earlier.

It was with a warmth in his heart and a (surprise!) pressure in his pants that he followed her downstairs where the babysitter was waiting. (Krissy was sulking, he recalled, because not only did she believe she was perfectly capable of doing the babysitting, she was horrified to be babysat.) But before they made it out the door, Anne handed the sitter her camera and pondered various possibilities for about five minutes before she grabbed Rob by the shoulders and posed him (a little more to the side, shoulders back, chin up) for the seven (just in case) shots she had the sitter take.

At dinner, Anne interrupted his heart-felt ramblings about how she looked and about what a nice anniversary it was, to give the camera to the manager (no mere server would do) and to instruct him in the proper way to capture the moment—the one she was currently ruining.

"Take a few shots, just to be sure," she'd said. The manager took four photos before Rob thanked him and gave Anne a warning look.

During the meal Anne sent back her soup as well as her halibut—one was not hot enough, the other simply "not quite right."

"Not quite right?" Rob said after the server left with her plate. "Who are you? *Goldilocks?*"

By that point Rob was still looking forward to Lyle Lovett, if not to anything else with his wife. Before they found their seats at the concert, Anne purchased a signed photo of Lovett as well as a bumper sticker over which she exclaimed, "Oh, this will be perfect for the Memory Book!"

Anne sat through the concert with a notebook in hand—like she was doing a review for the paper—jotting down the name of every song as soon as she recognized it. He didn't have to ask why she was doing it. They were doing the whole evening for one reason: the Memory Book.

"Will you jot down the next song for me?" Anne asked as she excused herself to go to the bathroom.

He deliberately wrote down the wrong song.

When that song came on during the encore, Anne looked at him suspiciously and he smiled. That's right: screw you and your memories.

But you don't mess with Anne's memories. Rob and Anne didn't speak the whole way home. Or the next day. And hardly the next. Things were even worse than they had been before their anniversary because she took the memory-stuff so personally, and he regretted that he'd allowed himself to be soft for a night.

Later when he saw the pages of their anniversary in the Memory Book, he was not shocked, for what could shock him anymore? There were heart stickers all around their photos—the two of them in front of the fireplace, at the restaurant, in front of the Lyle Lovett marquee—and block letter stickers announcing the date of their anniversary. Thirteen years, exclamation point. The bumper sticker she'd bought was placed vertically against the far right of the page, and the ticket stubs were used to frame the photo of them by the marquee. She detailed the "scrumptious" dinner they'd had, and there was the song list—rewritten—with a question mark where Rob had written the wrong song. In parentheses: "potty break," smiley face.

Ahh: Zoey.

Christmas Photo

Anne has one memory that is more real than the photo she recently found of it. She was four-and-a-half years old. In the picture she is standing between her two older brothers and her younger brother. The fourth and final boy was in her mother's belly. They were all in the living room in front of the record player. The boys were smiling and striking goofy poses in their nightshirts, while Anne stood slumped and somber in a full New York Giants uniform—shoulder pads, helmet, lace-up pants, jersey. She had believed the whole world (for her family was her whole world) had conspired against her to give her that football uniform for Christmas. Nick and Brian teased her about it. "I think Annie should get this!" "Don't you want your own football uniform, Annie?" Of course she hated it just like she hated all those blue, grey, and green toys in the boys' pages of the Sears Catalogue that were just like all the toys in their house. She wanted the pink stuff, the dress-up stuff, the girl stuff in the other part of the catalogue (which she almost never had a turn to look at). Most of all she wanted the Barbie mansion, which came with an elevator. Anne thought that if she agreed with whatever her brothers said about the stupid football uniform, they would shut up about it. It never occurred to her that they would follow through. Get her parents in on it. They could barely get through four innings of kickball without some major dispute breaking up the action.

But, there it was on Christmas morning, wrapped in an excitingly large box, and she innocently waited to open it last. She thought it might be the Barbie mansion, which was the only thing she'd written on her letter to Santa, lest he think she was giving him a choice. When she had waited as long as she could, she opened it slowly, savoring every last moment of unknowing. The box, brown cardboard with some writing she couldn't yet read (except for the letters, N, F, and L), did not reveal anything to her about its contents, though she was pretty sure it wasn't what she hoped. Then Brian jumped in and ripped the box open for her. It was all there at once for her to see, though in case she didn't, Nick was now helping as well, both boys pulling things from the box—jersey, pads, helmet—and laughing and laughing.

She stood as still as a snowman as Nick and Brian dressed her. The sound of Velcro, as they pulled the thigh pads tight around her too-skinny legs, attaching and reattaching until they held, was sandpaper scraping in her inner ear. The layers of hard plastic tapping against each other as her brothers pulled her arms and head through the shoulder pads was a hammer to her skull. One leg and then the other went through the pants; the queer shoelace tied at her waist. Then the jersey came over her head and hung from the shoulder pads like a scarecrow's shirt. When the helmet came on, she'd officially entered another world. She'd stuck her head inside of a shell and could hear the ocean roaring in her ears. Other sounds became muted. The helmet was too big, and her head bounced around inside it like the clapper of a bell. Her brothers pulled the chinrest and snapped it in place (the huge click-sound smacked her ear). She looked through the bars of the facemask at her family. Nick and Brian laughing, baby Patrick chasing the dog with a bow, her father watching the TV (now that the gifts were open), her mother picking up wrapping paper from the floor. "Help," Anne remembers saying.

"Take a picture! Take a picture!" her older brothers chanted.

The picture was taken. Anne's tears hidden by the helmet.

But in the moments that followed, Anne changed. The flash blinded her for a moment, and she blinked away her tears. As her brothers posed, one of them lost his balance and knocked her over. She fell, and even with him on top of her, she did not hurt. Baby Patrick jumped on them to join the fun of the tackle. That didn't hurt either. She lay there with the weight of her brothers shifting and pressing on top of her, and yet it was like being wrapped up in a sleeping bag. She could see the fading squares of the flash in the darkness of the helmet, and she got mad. At having her life run by boys. At her mother for letting it happen to herself and her daughter. At her weaknesses, all of them. In the chaos of the tackle-pile, and in the cushion of her pads, Anne fought back. She lunged her body left and right until her brothers were off of her. Then she rushed first against Brian—the eldest, the instigator—she took him by surprise and pegged him to the ground. Nick laughed and taunted her until she got up and lunged after him as well. His head hit the corner of bookcase, and he screamed when his hand felt blood. But Anne smelled the blood and went back after Brian, who was no longer laughing. This time she bent her helmet down and ran at him like a bull, aiming her thrust right where she'd heard that it counted. Brian bent over in pain and she jumped on his back, clutching his neck. At that point her father—whose voice she had been ignoring—pulled her off of Brian, carried her down the hall, deposited her on her bed, and shut the door with the instruction to come out when she was good and ready to apologize.

But Anne was not ready. Not even close. She began to do head-butts against her mattresses, then against her wall, then against her furniture. Each time she marveled that it did not hurt. The helmet banged around her head a bit, but there was no pain. She squared her shoulder against her dresser and pushed with all of her might until it moved six inches. Then she did it back the other way. She hit her thighs as hard as she could. The only thing that hurt was her hand.

From that point on, life got easier. Her brothers treated her with respect, and she treated them, as well as her parents, with none. She knew, intuitively, that she would be on her own in life. So be it.

Krissy's Babysitting Company

Krissy, interested though she is in her mom's business, is not interested in memories. She's not good at controlling them, like her mother is. The past is simply that which she has endured en route to the future. The present is that which she is currently enduring. The future, however, holds her attention. It is in her control. It changes however and whenever she wants it to. She thinks of it as a place, almost like heaven, where everything is perfect and feels right. But she knows that it will take hard work and good planning to get there—and that she will have to be tough. She thinks of her babysitting business as the first step toward her future.

But the present, being back at the Allens, is something she must endure. School is starting in two days, so she and Jared need to be close to home to catch their bus and have their clothes.

Krissy wants to put her plans into action, so she asks Mrs. Allen if she can take a walk.

Mrs. Allen looks at her doubtfully. "I don't know. All by yourself?"

Krissy looks at Mrs. Allen blankly. "Yes."

"Well, I suppose, but maybe just around our block, okay?"

"Okay."

Krissy goes straight to the Jennings' house. She is carrying her *Babysitter's Handbook.* She knocks on the door and two white-haired kids, Timmy and Joey, are pressing their faces against the glass door frame then glancing back toward the thudding sound Krissy can hear.

"Hello, Mrs. Jennings," Krissy says when the door opens. She is smiling and holding her head high. She is being tough. "I just wanted to let you know that I will be in sixth grade this year, and I am starting a babysitting company. I have been reading all summer about babysitting,"—here she holds up the book that has provided her with these lines—"and I would like to offer my services to you." She pulls out a perforated card from inside the book (the authors really thought of everything!) on which she has filled out her name and phone number and hands it to Mrs. Jennings.

"Why thank you, Krissy," Mrs. Jennings says. "I'll keep that in mind. And how's your mom doing?"

Krissy did not expect anyone else to know about her mother and she silently curses Mrs. Allen, who must have blabbed. She is doubly mad because she realizes she has no idea how her mother is. "She's okay," Krissy says.

"Will she be home soon then?"

Krissy doesn't know, but she doesn't want to let on. "Yeah, pretty soon."

Mrs. Jennings changes her tone. "And your father?" she says, as if it's a secret. "When will he be coming home?"

"Soon," says Krissy, who has no idea about this either.

Gossip

Anne is delighted when her neighbor Candace Coleman, who has agreed to take her home, winces at the sight of Anne and marvels that the hospital would let her go.

"I'm as shocked as you are," Anne is sure to repeat when one of the staff enters the room. When no nurses are around, she whispers to Candace, "I almost died," and nods with satisfaction at Candace's horrified expression.

"I'm pressing charges," Anne continues, leaving a lengthy pause before adding, "Attempted murder."

"What?" Candace says, shaking her head. "No. Rob? No."

"He tried to kill me, Candace. With the lamp."

"Oh my God," Candace says, and Anne can see that Candace's expression has begun to change. The eyes that have been so fixated on Anne have, without moving or looking way, begun to see through Anne, past Anne. To see something else entirely.

Anne begins to see something else as well—to see what will happen. Candace will get all the information and pass it on through the neighborhood. They—all of them—will feast like vultures on every dead meat detail and flock to Anne for more. Then, somehow, their natural interest in such intrigue will turn into something else. Fear? Disdain? Being the victim of attempted murder is, in the end, in a place like Brandenburg Estates, unacceptable.

Well, fine. Forget Candace. Anne will be getting the money, the house, the kids. Everything except Rob, whom she has had it with anyway.

Baseball Star

Rob has his own little mental Memory Book of his baseball days. His is better, he thinks, because he remembers sounds and smells, images in motion—not just some frozen snapshots, artificial poses with goofy titles, of things he wouldn't necessarily care to remember anyway.

He knows—and not just because Anne has told him—that it is, as she put it, "the epitome of selfishness" that he won't coach Jared's baseball team, but he believes that on the contrary, going to Jared's games at all is the most selfless act he commits. Every sensory experience—the spring grass smell, the crack of the bats, the sound of the umpire's call, the dirt tickling the hairs in his nose, the shuffling and cheering on the bleachers, etc., and etc., and etc.—takes him right back to the best days of his life. Then Anne yelling inane cheers (if Jared is in) or talking on her cell phone (if he's out), or his own potbelly resting on his thighs, reminds Rob that those days are long gone.

Rob regrets talking up his baseball years to Jared. He should've never mentioned them at all, should've let the kid get into wrestling or golf or something. But the problem he faced now was that Jared was good. Damn good. Without the benefit of Rob tossing with him. Without the benefit of decent coaches. Without hardly trying. He was simply and naturally good. He played third base because he was one of the few boys who could throw it accurately all the way to first. But they could put him anywhere on the field and he'd get the job done. Like his dad. But, unlike his dad, the boy could also bat. He didn't fall for the flabby pitches thrown by his opponents. He'd find the ball in or out of the strike zone and hammer a line drive between the basemen like he was threading a needle. The thing was, Jared didn't seem to care. Back in the spring, Rob finally addressed the situation directly.

"Son," he began. He cleared his throat and prepared to lower his voice. Jared was in the back seat, and they were driving home from a game. "It seems,"—minor throat clear—"It seems you've got a natural talent for baseball."

Rob tilted the rearview mirror just a bit so he could see part of Jared's face. Jared was looking at the car next to them at the traffic light. He made no reply.

"Well," Rob began again. "Do you think we ought to do something about it?"

"Like what?" Jared said, still looking out the window.

Rob accelerated. He dropped his father-son-talk voice for his sarcastic-impatient-dad voice. "Like get you on a better team with better coaches. Like practice together at home."

"No thanks."

"No thanks?"

"No thanks. I like my team."

"Don't you want to get really good? Maybe try to go pro?" Rob had not intended to suggest it because he never wanted Jared to do such a thing, but he also couldn't believe how apathetic Jared was being, so it came out.

Jared and Rob made eye contact in the mirror.

"No thanks."

"No, *thanks*? There's no *thanks* necessary, boy. I didn't just offer you ice cream. I asked what you want to do about baseball. Just *no* is fine."

"No," Jared said.

"That's more like it."

Money, Money, Money

Anne is surprised that the kids don't ask any questions about where their father is or what happened. But she is glad because she doesn't know what to tell them. It was one thing to tell Candace and Bridget (ultimately she couldn't resist sharing: their big neighborly eyes hypnotized her into it) about Rob posting bond and about her talks with a lawyer, but it was truly another to tell the kids. She let herself enjoy the feeling that Rob would not be coming home and bringing his oppressive aura into the house. She thinks of him in terms of cartoon characters: Eeyore, Pigpen. Eternally miserable; carrying a cloud of heaviness wherever he goes. Now she will tap into his bank accounts and live how she pleases.

How very nice of him to try to kill her.

What Anne finds, however, as she makes phone calls and accesses their accounts on the Internet, is that there is no money. Where the hell is all the money?

That night, after the kids go to bed early—tomorrow is the first day of school!—she calls the criminal at his parents' house, where he is staying until his cell is ready for him. "Where the hell is all the money?"

"What money?"

"Our money."

"*Our* money?"

"Where is it?"

"Well, let's see. *My* money just paid for bail. *My* money was put—by *you*—into updating a perfectly fine bathroom that no one ever uses anyway. Oh, and *my* money has stopped coming in while I await some sort of litigation. I should also mention that, pending prosecution, *my* money will cease to come indefinitely."

Anne hangs up on him to avoid revealing her surprise. No money in the accounts and no money coming in? She can't support two kids on Memory Books alone.

But where did all the money go? Yes, bail. Yes, the bathroom. But there was more money than that.

Rob Visits His Parents

Rob lies in bed in the room he grew up in. His baseball sheets, which replaced his *Star Wars* sheets, have since been replaced by a burgundy paisley comforter and matching pillow. His baseball awards are all in the closet with his posters and bulletin board. The walls have been painted taupe. His blood is boiling from his conversation with Anne, and he is sure he won't be able to fall asleep.

He is tempted to call Zoey, who has always been so good at helping him forget his problems. Life with Anne had become hard—not as in difficult, but as in rigid, petrified-like. He needed Zoey, her softness. She was such a jolt of carefree fun. At first, anyway. Now things were getting complicated, logistical. Now, he had to admit, she was part of the problem. She was living in a dump, and he couldn't feel good about her going from her car to her apartment alone (though she'd done it for three years now), so he sent her money, cash, to upgrade to a nicer place with a pool and on-site manager. But he couldn't keep going to Cleveland, and people at work were wondering about all these Cleveland-problems that couldn't be handled via the phone or computer. The plans were in the works to get her down to Cincinnati so they could see each other anytime. But the closer it came, the more he was afraid of Anne figuring it out. Which she did. And he'd gotten pissed about it because he didn't want to be forced to make a choice. For the most part he wanted the life he'd created with the kids and the house. And he wanted—needed—the release of Zoey. He didn't want to have to choose.

Home Sick, Part 1

Krissy skips the first day of school. She tells her mother, who looks like a total stranger and who Krissy therefore has no trouble lying to, that she is sick, and she spends the day in her room setting up her babysitting company, which, she has decided, is more pertinent to her future than school is. She brings her old dolls and stuffed animals up from the basement (avoids passing her mother), and names them after various children in the neighborhood. The old Cabbage Patch doll is Virginia. The lion and duck are Timmy and Joey Jennings. The moose is Randy Coleman. The unicorn is Susie Price. Kayla and Carrie Singleton are both bears. At first everyone is very well-behaved. Randy cuts his paw on a piece of paper, so Krissy—in accordance with her babysitting handbook—washes it with anti-bacterial soap, applies Neosporin, and places a band-aid on the wound. She comforts him, and when he seems ready, encourages him to resume play.

She is thinking about her dad, wondering if he's in jail (but too chicken to ask her mom), when Kayla and Carrie start to fight over whose turn it is at jacks. Kayla says Carrie didn't collect the right number of jacks, but Carrie insists that she did. Krissy strategically encourages them to perform a "do-over" and to proceed from there. She also warns them that if they fight again, they will not be allowed to play jacks for the rest of the day. She is proud of her ability to manage the conflict.

Susie thinks it is funny to poke her horn into Timmy and Joey's eyes. Timmy threatens to swallow her whole, and Joey says he will kick her with his webbed feet. Krissy hangs back hoping that they will solve their own conflict, but when Timmy lunges for Susie, she intervenes. She makes them discuss what happened and encourages Susie to apologize for acting out. Susie refuses to apologize, so Krissy removes her from the situation by asking her to perform a task. Susie will help change Virginia's diaper. While Krissy shows her how to do it, she inserts a few questions about Susie's actions with her horn.

"Place the new diaper under the one she's wearing so nothing gets on the table. That's it. Here's a wipe. Now, did one of those boys make you angry?"

"They knocked over my block tower."

This must have been while Krissy was dealing with Kayla and Carrie.

"That's it," Krissy says, encouragingly. "Now roll the diaper up with the wipe inside, and use the sticky tabs to close it up. Maybe next time something like that happens, you could come tell me first? Before you start poking people's eyes out?"

Krissy can't believe how well she is handling all these conflicts. She can never find her voice when her parents fight. She wishes her mom could see her.

"But," Susie protests.

"Not so loose," Krissy says. "You'll give her a saggy diaper. And no buts.

I want you to apologize, and I want them to apologize to you too."

"Them first!"

"The first to apologize is always the best."

Krissy is pleased to watch her charges exchange apologies and forgiveness, even if their heads are down and their voices so low as to hardly be audible. She rewards them with macaroni and cheese for lunch, plus a cookie.

Finally, it is naptime.

A Cup Of Coffee

It couldn't be. Anne is holding her coffee to her face, feeling the steam touch the sore surface of her eye, when she recalls Rob's various receipts and—despite the steam—turns cold with fear. His little Debbie or Daisy has it: the money.

Rob Considers The Children

Rob wakes up—which means he must have eventually fallen asleep—but does not rise from his bed. He can tell that it is late in the morning, and he knows that even though his parents, who have never really liked Anne, support him in his domestic struggles—which have suddenly turned into legal issues—they will find it unacceptable that he is still in bed. But he remains staring at the low ceiling, with its squeaky fan and pocked foam squares. He needs to call his lawyer, who had seemed less than optimistic on the telephone yesterday. "Unless you can get her to drop the charges," he'd said, "it's going to be a battle."

Rob ponders this notion of getting Anne to drop the charges. Unfortunately, the fact that he's been dipping deeper and deeper into the bank funds on account of his extramarital pursuits will not temper Anne's wrath any. To the contrary. His main hope—the trump card—is, as he's already suggested to Anne, the fact that if he goes to jail, she doesn't get any more money from him. But should he play this card, simply choosing one prison over another? Part of him is slightly thrilled by the idea of letting go of the image he's created for himself as a responsible, insurance-selling, suburbanite. Of just becoming a convicted felon, serving a few months in the big house, sustained by the visits of his devoted girlfriend, and then returning to society as a janitor or garbage man.

But he doubts his girlfriend would be quite so devoted to him if he were broke and in prison. And there are the kids to consider. Especially in times like this (not that there has been a time exactly like this before), when he is not with them, his love for them flares. For the images he holds in his mind of the kids are much like the images in Anne's Memory Books: static and ideal. He yearns for what it is they represent about life and family and love, about his own purpose and value. And he can't do this to them. He will fight to come home.

Home Sick, Part 2

Krissy—who was dreaming about her dad, something bad, but the specifics are taken from her—is woken abruptly by Timmy and Joey. Kayla is choking on a piece of popcorn. Krissy had not meant to fall asleep after she put everyone down for their naps, but she was exhausted from the morning. She is alert immediately. She sticks her finger down Kayla's throat to try to expel the popcorn. When it doesn't work, Krissy bends her over her knee and claps on her back. Kayla is still choking, but so silently. It is the other children that are screaming. Where had Kayla gotten popcorn? What was happening in her dream? Something about her dad. Something bad. But Kayla's eyes are huge with surprise and fear, and they are looking at Krissy, desperate. Like Krissy's father's eyes? She thinks she remembers that much of her dream—him looking at her like that. Now Kayla's face is changing colors. Krissy turns Kayla toward the wall and clutches around her waist, drawing her fists upward, as instructed by her handbook. But Kayla's body is soft and there is no resistance. And no sound. Choking should be loud, she thinks. Then she yells, "Call 9-1-1!" One of the boys picks up the phone and struggles to dial; his paws keep pushing two numbers at a time. Already it is getting too late. Kayla's eyes seem to be wider; now they are watering. But she is not moving. More time passes—precious time. Krissy tries again to swipe inside her mouth but Kayla's teeth come down upon her fingers. Within minutes that feel like seconds, or hours, Kayla is dead, and Krissy is rubbing the teeth marks in her skin.

Attempted Murder, Part 3

So. He gave the money—their money, her money—to the trixie.

Anne takes her pain-killers and looks at herself in the mirror to distract herself from such thoughts. From her temple down to her cheekbone and in the tender area just beneath her eye, the skin is purplish. Her eye is bloodshot. It's always a day or two later that bruises look the worst. Which makes this a perfect time to get that picture. She puts her digital camera on Rob's dresser so it is level with her, puts on the automatic timer, and positions herself for a photo. She reviews the image, then resets for a closer shot. This one will do.

Anne has made the room down the hall from kids' rooms into her Memory Book office. Here she keeps all of her supplies, neatly organized in labeled containers, along with her computer desk and assembly table. She'll bring Krissy some chicken noodle soup later; for now she'll let her sleep. Anne removes the memory card from the camera and inserts it into her computer tower so she can download the images. She loads her photo paper into the printer and sets up to print. While it prints, she tries to remember how she'd planned to design the page. She remembers the heading of course: *Attempted Murder*. And the general color scheme.

Anne would never put such a page into one of her Memory Books. But it soothes her very jumpy nerves to go through the process of creating the page. She actually has a secret box of such pages—*"Rage"* (when Rob threw a Bud Light bottle at the window over the kitchen sink, breaking the bottle and cracking the window, after she told him she didn't care if she ever had sex with him again), and even *"God's Wrath"* (when a lightning bolt struck a tree branch that fell right on the corner of the garage and the hood of their new SUV).

The ideas begin to flow as she sets red and black pages in front of her, as she files through her alphabet stickers. Her scissor drawer has over a dozen shears with various edge patterns, and she searches for the most jagged to use on her photo, which is nearly finished printing.

She is feeling better already, thinking more clearly. Now the money question is just that—a question to toss around in her mind while her body assembles the page. She holds various borders up against the background page, considers shapes, colors, placement. She gets her one-inch block cuts and counts out one for each letter in "Attempted Murder." Her photo has finished printing and when she gets up to retrieve it, she finds that her hands are shaking. Blames it on the caffeine, though her mind is thinking: The money is gone. The floozy has it.

"Preserve and Protect" had become a bit of a motto for her, like she was the commander-in-chief of a vulnerable country. She knew she would lose her status, security—her Memories—if she divorced Rob, so she didn't. But one little fight changed everything. She hadn't expected it to work out so perfectly, to look like attempted murder. So now she had the title, the new label of victim (she spells out the letters of this word in stickers even as she thinks it). But, just when she's free to divorce with dignity, the money is gone.

She works furiously to ward off images of living in the condos down the road, where everything was so pressed together, the decks and yards and living spaces a miniature version of what she has now. The kids sharing a bedroom; no room for her crafts. Creepy like a shrunken head.

Home Sick, Part 3

Oh god oh god oh god. In the chaos of Kayla's choking, the telephone cord got wrapped around Virginia's neck, and she too is choking, choking. Susie ran out to get help, but fell down the stairs where she lies in a broken heap. The bathwater is running, and Timmy is drowning. Where's the handbook?

Carrie is yelling at Joey. "Where have you been? What's her name?"

"None of your goddamned business!" Joey says.

"Oh yes it is my fucking business! Tell me!"

Joey grabs Krissy's lamp and swings it right at Carrie, who screams and falls to the floor.

Krissy cowers in the corner. She wants to stop them but she cannot move and no sound comes from her mouth. *Stop*, she mouths. *Say you're sorry.*

Mom, who is always so strong and competent, except when she's purple in the hospital, will shake her head in disapproval at Krissy's incompetence as a babysitter. No, worse, she will say she never expected anything else. Then Dad will swing the lamp at her. At Krissy? At Mom.

Even though she is not the type to curse—she thinks of it as a failure of imagination—Krissy curses at each one of her charges. She curses them individually and ends with a sweeping, *Damn you all to hell!* They have ruined her future, everything. She will never get paid, never be trusted. She is ruined. Ruined.

She is clutching the horn of the dead unicorn when she gets an idea that will require all the strength, all the toughness, she can muster: Cover her tracks. Make it look like an accident.

A Deal Is Made

The phone is ringing. Anne goes downstairs to refill her coffee and to answer the telephone.

Rob's father's name appears on the caller-ID. "What do you want?"

"I want to make you an offer," Rob says.

"Forget it," she says, though she hesitates before hanging up.

"It's about money."

She pours her coffee. "Go ahead," she says, when she is good and ready.

Anne listens as Rob tells her about giving his little Mindy or Molly a bunch of money that he can't get back. (Just as Anne suspected, the girl was trailer trash. She bites her tongue, hard.) She listens to his sob story about the kids, and only wishes, as he approaches his predictable proposition, that she would have the strength to refuse him.

Anne repeats his offer for clarity. "You break it off with this . . . *girl*," she says, though many other terms come to mind. "You go back to your job and get your full income with which we will replenish our accounts. *Our* accounts. You come back to the house. I drop the charges."

"Correct," he says.

Anne eyes the rows of Memory Books on the bookcases by the fireplace. Aside from the money, she does not want to lose the Memories. Aside from the Memories, she does not want to lose the money.

"Fine," she says through clenched teeth. "Whatever."

"Good. When can I come home?"

An Accident

The matches are in the bathroom. In her room Krissy strikes a matchstick briskly along the chalky red stripe, holds the flame to the frayed fur of a tail, watches it flare and singe. Strikes another, and touches it to the fringe of curtain, which takes the flame nicely. As does her bedskirt. And her fresh stack of school supplies—five pocket folders, 200 sheets of looseleaf. Across the floor she sees *The Complete Babysitter's Handbook* and crawls to it. She consults the Table of Contents one last time, and sure enough, nothing. Not one helpful thing. Be sure to have a list of telephone numbers in case of emergency. Your first priority in babysitting is to keep the kids safe. Do you know how to change a diaper? She sets every last useless word on fire. No one will never know that it was all her fault, that she was unable to make them behave, that—here she struggles a bit as she tries to breathe—that she was unable to stop things from getting—

Homecoming

As he drives, Rob sheds the dead skin of Zoey, of his parents, of prison, of secrets. The stores taper off to a cluster of car dealerships, and after he turns right at the Superamerica, he is surrounded by trees, by a patch of corn, by a new development of homes, then another, then his own. He sees the welcoming sign of his neighborhood, named after an English manor, and feels quite like a gentleman of an English manor. He drives slowly through the streets, rolls down the windows, and enjoys the warmth of the late-August day (though it is *awfully* warm, so he also keeps on the A/C), the deep green colors of the trees and grass, and the sight of toddlers having free reign over the sidewalks and driveways now that their school-aged siblings are away for the day. He waves to a cute young mother in overall shorts. When did *she* move in?

A sprinkler splashes the side of his car and several drops touch his face through the open window. He laughs out loud; he is practically giddy. Rob drives slowly, like a hero on parade, like the freaking ice cream man.

He inhales deeply, taking in all the beauty and perfection of his world.

But he shakes his head and makes a face, for something dark and dirty fills his nose, which tingles and burns.

He turns onto his own street.

Fire

Anne passes her favorite framed photo of the family and is assured of her decision. She opens the garage door and waits for Rob. What's that smell?

Fire

Something is wrong. He's almost there. Everything looks okay. Just a weird feeling. Then he is in front of the house and something in the upstairs window—or is it a reflection? He slams into the mailbox.

Fire

—so out of control—the smoke the smoke the—

MERMAIDS

"Nothing gave her so much pleasure as to hear about the world above the sea."
—"THE LITTLE MERMAID," HANS CHRISTIAN ANDERSEN

I.

The birthday girl begins her day with a question: "Do wishes really come true?"

She is using a plastic knife to spread blue icing along one side of her cake.

The birthday girl's mother, at work on the other side of the cake, wonders why she asks.

Because the birthday girl doesn't think they do. For she has wished upon stars and eyelashes and last year's birthday candles and pennies in the fountain, and she has not told anyone (except for her doll, Annabelle, and her unicorn, Chloe) her wish—it is always the same one—and it still has not come true.

"Do they?" She asks again, pausing from her work.

The birthday girl's mother says that sometimes they do and sometimes they don't and that it just depends.

The birthday girl wants to know on what it depends.

The birthday girl's mother looks at her. "On how much it costs, on whether it's even possible—that kind of thing."

Which brings the birthday girl to another question. She plunges her knife into the icing container. "Are mermaids real?" she says.

The birthday girl's mother hesitates. Between them on the table is a plastic figurine of Ariel, the Little Mermaid, whom they will set atop the cake, iced like the bottom of the sea. All over her daughter's room are images of Ariel, with her red hair and green fish tail and eyes the size of the shells on her breasts.

For some time she has wanted to tell her daughter not that mermaids aren't real—that would be too simple—but that Ariel isn't real, that there is another, better mermaid story. She has thought to tell her daughter that what the real Little Mermaid wanted was not the prince but an immortal soul. That the real Little Mermaid never even married the prince. That when it became clear the prince would marry another, she could have killed him to save her own life, but she tossed the knife into the sea. Strangely, instead of dying, she was taken by the Daughters of the Air, who spread health and the perfume of flowers around the world. The birthday girl's mother has wanted to tell her daughter that the real Little Mermaid became a Daughter of the Air, able—unlike her merman family who would live for three hundred years and then turn to foam—to earn an immortal soul.

The birthday girl challenges her mother's silence with a statement of the evidence: Mermaids are in stores and movies and books; here is one in front of them. What could be more real?

They both look at Ariel, her stiff, curvy body tipped awkwardly on the tabletop. Ariel wears an expression of feigned and deceptive innocence, and the birthday girl's mother wants to diminish her appeal.

"No, sweetie," she says, looking straight into Ariel's eyes. "Mermaids are not real." And then, in a moment that feels like inspiration, she adds, "Besides, mermaids can't ride bicycles!"

She watches for her daughter's response. Later today, her daughter will find a bicycle topped with a bow awaiting her in the garage, and the birthday girl's mother thinks how perfect it would be if she could get her daughter to wish for a bicycle, rather than to be a mermaid.

But then again, she thinks, isn't it better for her daughter to learn that wishes don't always come true?

She becomes aware that she is once again complicating something that is actually quite simple. That is what her husband would say. "Stop making things more difficult than they are," he would say if he were there. That, or, "Keep it simple, stupid."

But he is out getting the bicycle.

The birthday girl takes another angle. "Are unicorns real?" she asks.

That's when the birthday girl's mother realizes that her daughter's line of questioning is going beyond mermaid wishes, and into, well, ontology. And she suddenly longs for the days of diapers and bottles, which had overwhelmed her at the time with their relentlessness and which she'd been relieved to finally move beyond, and which seemed, now, so mindlessly simple. If the diaper stunk or swelled up, she changed it. If her daughter cried a few hours after her last feeding, she fed her. Now her daughter wants to know if her playmates are real. If wishes come true.

The birthday girl's mother makes a decision: to keep it simple.

"No," she says. "Unicorns are not real."

"Are princesses real?" the birthday girl asks.

The birthday girl's mother tells her that there were princesses in the past and that there are still some princesses in other countries, but that they are different from the princesses she knows about.

The birthday girl wants to know which countries, but her mother doesn't know. And she's not about to mention Diana.

"Is Elmo real?"

She is told he is a puppet with a human voice.

Then the birthday girl wants to know if Michael, the blond boy on *Barney*, is real.

"He is a real person, but his name is not Michael, and he's probably twenty-one by now."

The birthday girl is quiet. She sullenly jabs the cake with her knife, and the birthday girl's mother begins to question her approach.

See? She finds herself arguing with her husband in her head. *I don't make things complicated. Things are complicated.*

But the birthday girl is persistent. She tries again. "Are pilgrims real?" For she has just learned about them in kindergarten.

"Yes!" Her mother is finally able to say. "Pilgrims are real!"

But, no, the birthday girl cannot see one because they were real a long time ago.

"Is the Tooth Fairy real?"

"Is Benjamin Franklin real?"

"Is Scooby Doo real?"

"Is heaven real?"

The birthday girl's mother looks at her daughter, who, herself, was not real, not even imagined, merely six years ago. And even though the birthday girl's mother watched her own stomach grow, and felt and witnessed the slick being emerge from within her, and even though she has also witnessed each day of her daughter's life, the child's very existence seems more fantastically impossible than that of any unicorn or mermaid. She has at times reached out to touch her daughter—stroked her hair, squeezed her hand—just to know she has not dreamed her.

She reaches out to her daughter now to wipe some icing from her cheek. She lets her daughter lick it from her finger. "Let me finish the cake," she says. "You go get dressed for your party."

II.

The birthday girl has chosen to have her party at Chuck E. Cheese Pizza, and at the door the birthday girl's mother is assaulted by pops and thwacks and dings, by primary colors alight and blinking, by the kinetic energy of other people's children, and she is relieved to simply receive a stamp on her hand, to smile at the teenager who has stamped her, to push the turnstile, and to release the birthday girl's hand.

The extended family arrives, and while the grandparents help themselves to slices of buttery pizza, the birthday girl's mother divvies out tokens to cousins who stand—or bounce—before her in socks, their sneakers hastily crammed into the nearby shoe rack. They are like the parts of the game nearby that pop-up one at a time, and she imagines, for a moment, hitting them over the head with the rubber hammer. She shudders a bit when they call her "Aunt."

She turns her attention to the cake and gifts. Ariel is smiling up at her from the blue sea beneath the saran-wrap, and she glares back at her before pushing the cake against the wall. The candles and film, she realizes, are still on the kitchen table. She sends her husband, who reminds her of all the errands he's already run today, to the nearest drug store, and then she stands alone beneath the tunnels of tubes and follows the path of her daughter, who stops at a small window, waves, and crawls away. She admits to herself that she is avoiding her in-laws, afraid, somehow, of their simple happiness, and afraid of ruining it.

But unavoidable are the other mothers, all around her, who look so at home in this unreal place which can only rightly be called a giant mouse cage, what with the children crawling through a maze of tubes, with all the cheese, and with, well, the mouse. These mothers travel in packs, maintaining conversations, and even eye contact, despite the toddlers slung on their sides thrusting sippy-cups in their faces. They carry wipies everywhere they go and remembered to call ahead for their children's parties, which are now set up at long tables in the adjacent room (and not, like her daughter's, in crammed booths by the games), and where their children watch as fuzzy mechanical robots jerk their arms and turn their startling faces to the right and left to stripped-down and abridged versions of last year's pop songs, and where Chuck E. first emerges from his mouse hole to mingle with the children.

She should, she thinks, tell her daughter to ask these mothers her questions. They look like women with answers.

The birthday girl pops out of the bottom of one of the slide tubes, spies an older cousin, and follows her back up the climber.

The birthday girl's mother knows that she cannot continue to stand here, alone amid the darting children, that she must return to the adults, that she must smile. But she feels a headache coming on. The colors, the noise, the kids. It is like too many exclamation points. Why, she suddenly, or perhaps constantly, wonders, hadn't her own wishes come true? On what had it all depended? How had she ended up in this unfamiliar, even unreal, life? She hadn't, like her daughter, wished to be a mermaid. She had not wished for the impossible.

Strange, she thinks, how the Little Mermaid—the real Little Mermaid—fell in love with the prince and longed to be a human with an immortal soul. But the poor creature—half-human, half-fish—ended up neither on land nor sea, but in the air. She became a Daughter of the Air, dependent, for her immortal soul, upon (of all things) the deeds of children. A child's good deed would bring her to heaven one day sooner. But a bad deed would add a day to her mortal trials.

Perhaps this is what happens to all wishes: some partial rendering, some unnatural transformation. It might explain her being here now.

Her eyes begin to burn, and everything starts to look like it's underwater, like a coral reef, where everything fits perfectly into a system—a school of fish here, a colorful rock there—except her. She was not made for this environment. She cannot breathe here.

But she will not cry. Not about her in-laws (and certainly not in front of them) or about the other mothers or about the birthday girl's father (who had always and simply been wrong), or about the possibility that this life might be all her soul ever knows.

Suddenly Chuck E. is in the main room, and there is the birthday girl hugging and then staring at the six-foot tall smiling mouse, mesmerized. Unable to capture the moment with a photo, the birthday girl's mother kicks herself for forgetting the film and candles (and everything else she has forgotten and will forget to do as a mother), and prays that Chuck E., who is rubbing and patting her daughter's back, is not really a pervert pretending to be a mouse (just as she is a—what?—pretending to be a mother), and she considers, for a moment, whether it would be better to tell her daughter, who will soon make another wish upon her birthday candles, that Chuck

E. and his world of tickets and prizes are not real, that this world of people gathering to celebrate her and her birthday is not really how the world is or ever will be again. But then she looks around at the chaos of colors and shapes, and bends down, spreading her arms like wings, to receive her daughter who has come to hug her and to gush about Chuck E., and she feels her daughter's arms around her neck, pressed against the base of her hair, feels the gentle puff of her daughter's breath against her cheek, and she feels herself being lifted, up and away. When she moves her legs, she finds herself floating up faster, effortlessly, as if through water. She does not touch the ceiling, and yet she is past it, in the air, where she can breathe again. She is flying, outstretched, like a gull above the sea. She calls down to her daughter—and it comes out a song.

"Be good," she cries, for she knows her soul will depend upon it.

TOM'S STORY

The first sentence of the story establishes the fact that the main character is Tom and that he's having a bad day. No mention is made of Gina in the first sentence. The next sentence provides dialogue in which Tom tells someone—the reader does not know whom yet—to fuck off. "'Fuck off,'" it says that he says. At this point, it is revealed that the person addressed is Gina, that she is Tom's girlfriend, and that she has begun to cry.

A suggestion of conflict having been economically established, a brief description of the setting follows, locating Tom and Gina on a couch in Tom's apartment. Clues are provided to suggest that they have spent a great deal of time on this particular black leather couch with its large tear on one side and in this particular apartment, especially at this particular time of the evening when sunlight drains from the room as if there were some sort of leak. It may even be implied that the tension between the couple is either nothing new or has been mounting for some time. While the reader forms a still image of the scene of Tom—slouched, sprawled, and unshaven, staring at the muted TV—and of Gina—looking at Tom and maintaining a protective self-embrace—the narrative introduces Rusty, who has conveniently arrived on the scene. Rusty is described as a mostly-cocker-spaniel mutt with a good sense of timing. The latter information is not intended ironically, for at the literal level of the story Tom is pleased by the dog's arrival and leans forward to tug on its ears, but succeeds on its potential to be understood as such.

By this point it is clear that the narrator is not omniscient, but is limited to Tom's perspective, and that the account of the situation will be obviously biased and probably distorted by Tom's emotional state. That the narrator will not claim to be Tom (through the use of "I") but only to speak for him, the clever reader will recognize as dissembling, for how can someone who knows the perspective of only one person be anyone other than said person? Less experienced readers, however, will conflate character, narrator, and author, and believe that "Tom" is just a substitute for the author himself, even if the story is written by a woman. In which case, they will think she must be a lesbian, a *tom*boy, and that "Gina" is a deliberately shortened form of a word they prefer not to say aloud. (These are not the worst type of readers. At least they are trying.)

Rusty's timely entry upon the scene has allowed for a shift in perspective—in Tom's perspective, that is, as his attention moves from Gina (who has recently gotten an unflattering haircut and who he wishes would stop staring at him with that needy look on her mug) to his apartment and to the dog. The narrative begins to reveal, through thoughts prompted by specific objects within his view (Rusty's food bowl, the beat-up mountain bike, a pile of video games and cords, a table cluttered with used dishes and unopened mail), the failures and frustrations of Tom's thirty-two years. Tom continues to pet Rusty—admitting to himself (according to the narrator, who claims not to be Tom) to being calmed by the repetitive movement and the soft fur but unnerved by Gina's relentless stare—as he surveys the stuff of his quotidian existence with a feeling more of sad regret than the anger suggested in the opening lines. That his current feeling is regret rather than the suggested anger is not a flaw in the narrative's beginning, a red herring, a false clue; it is a true (the limitations of "truth" notwithstanding) reflection of a change, if only temporary, in Tom's mood.

It is revealed, in a long stream-of-consciousness-like narrative paragraph, that what has made this the day, as Tom has decided, to fully and finally break things off with Gina (besides it being a necessary action for the narrative drive of the story) is that earlier in the day he drove by the cross on the side of the highway—the one that he's never been able to turn away from, the one that means he has been spared, the one, in short, that has his name on it—and realized that it has been ten years: Ten years since the Thomas-who-was-not-him died. Ten years since Tom, our protagonist, first drove by the bright white cross and saw his own name intersecting the numbers of the current year. Ten years (this phrase is repeated in this way, for effect) since he promised himself that Thomas (may he rest in peace) would not die in vain, but that he (the dead Thomas) would live on as an Inspiring Spirit (here Tom smiles at the term he employed at the time, Inspiring Spirit), as a motivational force for Tom, who would be graduating from college that long-ago June, and who had little more planned than the smoking of vast quantities of pot. Tom had made, the story says, a pact with himself (he even devised a ritual involving candles and the wee-est bit of blood) to do something great enough that he would be able to tell the world about the other Thomas, who had died prematurely (though Tom was not sure by how much for he did not know anything about Thomas except that he was dead) and tragically (obviously a car accident), and who had remained with him (Tom) as an Inspiring Spirit. But instead of fulfilling his personal pact, it is explained, all those years ago Tom met Gina and subsequently did nothing.

In a new paragraph more information is provided about the ten-year period and how specifically Tom managed to ruin it, along with details that allow the reader to question whether Tom had in fact blown it completely or whether (as is often the case) the character is simply not appreciating what is right in front of him: Gina, who is still, Tom can tell out of the corner of his eye as the present situation resumes, staring at Tom and hugging her shins. Just then a scene not in the story but on the television distracts Tom. It is a commercial with several dozen employees of a local company standing and smiling and waving at him in over-bright sunlight in front of their workplace, their long shadows stretching behind them like phantoms.

"'Do you see that?'" It says that he says.

It then says that he looks at Gina (who really needs to keep her hair longer), then back to the TV. Creeped out by the smiles, the shadows, the flapping hands that might cause the entire group to fly away or cause a windstorm, Tom, it says, temporarily softens to the familiarity of Gina and all their years together and considers apologizing for the earlier fuck off comment.

It becomes clear that Tom does not apologize, for there follows another paragraph of Tom's thoughts, which appear to be unmediated by the third-person narrator. Tom thinks (without it saying that he thinks) of what he will do if he never gets to tell anyone about Thomas, about the Inspiring Spirit who led him to such greatness. Then he thinks—with no little sense of fury or amazement—that perhaps everything is Thomas's fault after all. If he (Thomas) had been a more *Inspiring* Spirit, Tom might not be stuck where he was. He (Tom) might be something, something worth proclaiming, if Thomas had really stuck with him. Then Tom makes eye contact with Rusty and it occurs to him that things did start to improve all those years ago when he found Rusty, or was found, as these things go. Life, Tom decides, definitely got better then, shortly after he'd made the pact. He recalls, for example, that he started drinking less. Perhaps, Tom concludes, Thomas did come to him after all: in the form of Rusty. The narrator offers no commentary on whether this is a logical train that has perhaps veered off track. On the contrary, even remarkably, Rusty begins to lick Tom's hand at that very moment, lending credence to Tom's new theory as well as to his belief in Rusty's uncanny sense of timing—both of which now seem related.

The narrator returns to tell the reader that Tom feels re-inspired, that he is prepared to make changes, to make up for lost time. (Nothing specific is mentioned in this regard.)

The reader (who has anyway checked the length before committing to the piece, and who even now spies the field of white space beyond the dense woods of words) senses that the story is approaching, if not a resolution, an end. The reader is not necessarily optimistic, not about Tom or the story.

Tom stares at and pets Rusty until the reader, who has remembered Gina's presence even if Tom seems to have forgotten, wonders why Tom doesn't tell Gina everything. She seems like a good listener. The reader may even sense the potential dramatic power in an ending which shows Tom embracing Gina as his greatest success (even his only one) and symbolically making *her* the dreamed-of audience for his tale of Thomas.

Instead, Tom looks over at Gina, and she is described as trying to smile. Tom, it is said, finds both her gesture, which does little more than reveal a piece of spinach in her teeth, and her haircut, which needs no further comment, pathetic. A carefully crafted sentence informs the reader that Tom's reaction to Gina's smile and haircut is a simple displacement of the fact that he cannot love and respect a person who loves and respects a person such as himself. He should, Tom concludes, find a woman who will find him intolerable until he makes something of himself.

A further implication is made that Gina would never understand the business about Thomas and about Tom's failures—but that the reader would. That this is why the story is being told at all.

But a clever reader, though flattered, will observe in this, the conclusion of the story, that the perspective has shifted to a restrained omniscience, which describes Rusty turning away from Tom for a quick nibble on his own crotch, and Gina, who is no longer crying, who seems in fact quite done with crying, rising from the couch and casting a shadow from the kitchen light over Tom's face, her own head surrounded by a hazy glow. It seems that while Tom, the narrator, and the reader have been caught up in Tom's story, Gina has been on the terrifying and exhilarating edge of turning a new leaf, of starting a new chapter (book-based metaphors intended) in her own life. She has a great new haircut, for instance, one she's wanted for years. (Here she touches the edge of her hair where it strikes her neck; she loves the feel of the fresh cut against her soft skin.) This is it, she thinks, it's really over. She feels tall and powerful standing above Tom. Though she's not moving at all, she feels inside like one of the people in the commercial that was just on, smiling and gesticulating ecstatically with full arms, waving farewell. Tom, she thinks, can curse if he needs to; she knows that deep down he doesn't mean it. Sometimes he speaks harshly without thinking, or speaks carelessly when he's thinking about weird things (which he is obviously doing again) and doesn't know what he's saying. "Goodbye, Tom," she is thinking sadly and with respect for their ten years together, but she is also thinking, "And good riddance." She does not say any of this, however, and the story is back in Tom's perspective so the reader remains unaware of anything other than her expression of—*Could it be pity?* The very possibility makes Tom curse again.

In the end the reader is left to decide whether to accept the final image in which, though no doors have been opened or sound made, Gina simply disappears from the scene, from the story, and from Tom's life—leaving Tom on the couch alone and still, somehow, in her shadow. Or whether to reject such a physical impossibility as a meaningless trick of narrative.

FORTNIGHT IN D MINOR

My daughter's hair was in a low ponytail. I lifted the scissors to the elastic band and she began to cry.

"It's your fault," she said, referring to the crying, to the fact that I too get disproportionately emotional about some things.

The haircut wasn't my fault. It was her idea, and no one was forcing her to do it. I put the scissors to my own hair and cut off an inch or two at the neck. From the tiny bouquet in my fingers I could tell I'd cut it at a bad angle. I adjusted the mirrors so I could see the back of my head. Yep, uneven. I cut again.

"Okay," she said, taking a deep breath. "Ready." Then she saw her long-haired reflection and started crying again.

<hr />

When I was ten my mother gave me a perm. My hair was about two-feet long, fine, and straight. It took many hours to roll each piece into the plastic roller and fix it to the top of my head. I wonder what my mother and I talked about all that time. I wonder if she said, I am not happy, I have not been happy for a long time. To which I might have said, Happy? I understood the term no better then than I do now. But perhaps my mother said, I'm pregnant, since my brother was born that same year. Or: In three years I will leave your father.

<hr />

"Mom!" my daughter called from the bathroom. She liked her haircut, by the way. This was days later. "*Mom!*"

"Here, Poof." I tossed a sock ball to the cat. "Coming!"

The door was open like a loose tooth, and I stepped into its abscess.

"It's shorter," she said, eyeing her several reflections in the angled mirrors, a growing tremor in her voice. "It's up to my chin," she said of her hair. "You cut it to my shoulders but now it's up to my chin."

I pulled on a section, which snapped up like an elastic when I let go. Now it was up to her ear. Poof rubbed against my leg and meowed.

"Someday you'll laugh about this," I said, and began to cry.

>⟶

My permed hair resulted in about twelve inches of limp waves weighing down twelve more inches of straightness. What more could you expect of a home perm back then? I expected more nonetheless. My mother took a picture of me standing outside squinting into the sun, as if to document the moment I learned that nothing will ever work out like I want it to.

My baby brother was healthy and smart, everyone agreed. Today he is unhealthy (half asthma, half cigarettes), his intelligence underused.

My mother is dead.

>⟶

By the weekend my daughter was completely bald. Her hair did not fall out like you might think. Instead each strand disappeared into the pores of her scalp like a piece of spaghetti sucked between hungry lips.

Talk about crying.

"There, there," I said, patting her smooth head, though all I could think was, Where, where?

>⟶

True, I haven't mentioned her father. I left my daughter's father before he could ring me. Had I waited a dozen or so years to leave him, there would have been no surprise. My father certainly wasn't surprised when my mother left.

But the surprise was on me. I did not know my daughter's father was my daughter's father because I did not know anything about a daughter sprouting inside me.

They grew together over the months: my daughter, the lie. Then the years.

>⟶

Monday morning she woke up and what was she doing? Not crying and begging me to homeschool her. She was painting the world on her bald head. First a layer of blue ocean. Then cuts of greenish-brown adjoining pork chops around the left ear, North and South America.

"Here," she handed me an eyeliner pencil when I walked in. "You do Siberia."

Siberia is where her father died while on a scientific expedition. She is brave like him.

><

Without hair my daughter was a new life form. Everyday she came home from school with a group of small people orbiting her. Everyday she and her galaxy of friends would create a new image on her head. A snow globe. A tennis ball, basketball, soccer ball. An ice cream sundae. A Siberian tiger.

"I've never felt so close to Dad," she said with a yawn one night when I tucked her in. She still lets me do that sometimes.

><

For a week I slept fitfully. In my dreams my daughter was always staring at me with unblinking Siberian tiger eyes and walking the wrong direction.

><

It was not hard to find her father. Not in this day and age.

"You have a daughter," I said into the phone. "You have," but it was still ringing, "a daughter."

It rang one more time and when a woman answered it I hung up because she didn't have a daughter. Or if she did it was a different one.

I called again later and this time he answered. "You," I said. Then my voice failed.

"Hello?"

My daughter, our daughter, was practicing her violin in the next room. "Hello?" he said several times. Then he finally stopped asking Hello and just listened to his daughter's Minuet in D Minor all the way until the end. I held the phone for a long time after I hung up.

＞￢ー

Every night for two weeks we did that. A fortnight. I called and she played and he didn't say hello just listened and I hung up. Then I held the phone. That's how I thought of it, as one thing, our fortnight.

Many things can happen in a fortnight. A girl can correct her fingering until she plays a piece almost perfectly. A violin's notes can prick through a person's heart and spin through veins like iridescent silk. And another person's, and another's. And the three can be sewn together as if they were never apart.

Or stitched up like an open wound.

＞￢ー

Or.

＞￢ー

My daughter's hair has grown back and some of the friends disappeared like extinguished stars and others remain a part of her galaxy and her laughter is like a comet and what would I have said to him anyway? You could never live up to the Siberian explorer she believes you to be? She thinks her crying is from me and her bravery is from you, but her bravery is only from the stories of you? Which makes it from me after all.

A fortnight, would I have said, is better than a baker's dozen marriage that hardens and molds before her eyes?

"What's wrong, Mom?" My daughter sets down her violin and hugs me while I hold the empty phone and cry.

FALLING

She lies—a word that depends heavily on the word that follows—in (of course in, she lies in something, not about something, not to someone, for that would make her a liar, and she is not that, except to herself sometimes) the middle of the bed beside her quote-unquote Boyfriend of seven months, whom she fell for (as if she did it for him, on his behalf) immediately, but who refuses to call her his Girlfriend for reasons, she is sure, other than the fact that he is thirty-eight (several years older than she) and too old, as he says, to have a Girlfriend, which, she argues, is merely semantics, and though no one loves language, loves semantics (the way a word's meaning shifts and changes around other words, the way a word—like a person!—means one thing here, another there) more than she, his quibbling seems somehow silly, so she spoons (the verb!), pressing her body against his until she begins to fall (or was she already falling) asleep, but as she falls deeper into sleep (as if sleep were merely a holeintheground into which one falls deeper and deeper, and not the most PERFECT DIMENSION where everything is made of words that need only be spoken to be real), she rolls, as she falls (she must admit that it does feel quite like falling), away from her Boyfriend, which she calls him anyway (when he's not around), and faces the other side of her bed, where—*could it be?*—her Ex-Husband, whom she divorced in A State of Desperation and Panic after only two years of marriage and whom she misses (terribly!) but has resolved (firmly!) to live without, is, and he's wondering why she's with the Boyfriend—*at least someone's not afraid of the term!*—and in reply she grunts, which her Ex-Husband (who always understood her completely) understands completely and to which he adds (he always knew just what to say), "When you should be with me," but she has already ruined things with him by falling apart so utterly and leaving the way she did, which pissed off His Mother who will never forgive what was done to her son, and so she says *quite aloud*: "But what about Your Mother?"—which causes the Boyfriend (for, really, what else is there to call him?) to roll over and say, "What *about* my mother?"— and to which she absently replies with a light pat on his forearm, "Don't worry, not *your* mother," before turning back with full attention to her Ex-Husband, who is still there, or not there, and she thinks of how she wishes she could undo the mistakes she made when she was young and freaked out about living in a Ranch House on a street called Valley Wood Road adjacent to Forest Hill Road adjacent again to Brook Farm Road, where every word was a noun except for the ones disguised as adjectives, and about having to do alliterative things like Weeding on Weekends (With The Mother), and about Starting a Family, which, though not Alliterative At All was no less terrifying, and which all of her friends are doing now, five years later, and which she would like to do more than anything, but which is hard to do when your Boyfriend won't even call you his Girlfriend not to mention Wife, but, alas, she can't undo what she did back then (she can't unfall apart or even fall together), and even if she could make things O.K.—*but what do these letters stand for?*—with her Ex-Husband (and right now, as she falls deeper into sleep, it seems entirely possible that she can), she could never make them O.K. with His Mother, and it could never be the way it was, for she would be instead like Hester Prynne with a Scarlet Letter—perhaps, why not, her own initial "D"—that stood for something like Deserter, Destroyer, Dumbass (The Mother would have, no doubt, *unlimited* suggestions), and even though, in her bed, in her sleep, and always, she, the X-Wife (as in Wife with an X through it), was sorry, as repentant as she could be (which, by the bye, Hester Prynne never was), and even though she still loves her Ex-Husband and fears she always will, there is just no undoing the past, and eventually she falls (she thinks) asleep, sleeps restlessly, and so wakes up groggy (one of her favorite words, but only when it doesn't describe her), and it occurs to her the next day, the next morning—it must still be morning, the Boyfriend always leaves first thing in the morning, even when it is raining and she asks him to stay—it occurs to her then, soon after the Boyfriend has gone home, when she is standing at her sink watching last night's dishes and washing the cold rain—no, wait, washing dishes, watching rain, cold rain—fall (it's the only thing rain can do, fall, like she does, fall for the Boyfriend, fall asleep, fall apart, why is she always) on the naked November trees (this late in fall all leaves have fallen), it occurs to her then, after the Boyfriend has gone home—but this has been said already, how he always leaves first thing in the morning, even when she is falling and she asks him to stay—that, oh! how it catches her (offguard) catches her (unawares) catches her (breath), that: No one else, not the Boyfriend or the Ex or the Mother, can break her (fall) for she is free (falling) and something stronger than even silicone-nylon is unfolding within her, ready to explode overhead, hold tight the air, and ease her gently, safely down.

LENT

Lent should be in the summer that she might make use of the motel pool, bandaged up outside like an open wound. She never had a pool. She had a cat but her cat is dead. Buried in leftover snow behind the garage until the ground softens. It would be nice to swim in a pool. But then she remembers: I am Jesus in the desert! No swimming allowed.

I am giving you up, she told her family. For Lent.

What was hers anymore that she could give up? That no one else could use without permission, take without asking, even wear, now that the oldest was a teen and her size? Answer: the cat. The found feral cat from college, from before all of them and during all of them, tucked into the right angle of her armpit every night. But after they started arriving every couple years, the cat (may she rest in peace) was no longer her greatest joy. They were.

You are my greatest joy, she said. And so, she addressed the question marks around the dinner table, you see what a sacrifice this is.

Of course they didn't believe her. They never really knew how to read her. She complained of being an old lady one day and ran around making snow angels the next. She occasionally referred to her children as parasites, but cried every time she read The Giving Tree. This Lent thing was obviously a joke. Except it wasn't. She'd been doing research, Googling "lent," Googling "lenten sacrifice," Googling "motel reservations." Here, she said, producing a receipt. She'd printed it off of Travelocity and scratched out the motel name and address but not the city, which was the same one they lived in. You're going to stay right here in town, they said. I'm not giving up my whole life, she told them. Just you.

Her husband neither commented nor protested, for he knew his wife better than the children did but not, perhaps, as well as he thought. I'm giving up Starbursts, the youngest declared.

On Fat Tuesday, Mardi Gras, she could not get enough of them. She made a feast, played Xbox 360 with her son and dress-up with her youngest, and talked, like, omigod, for hours with her teen. Late that night she went down on her husband, who was pretty sure he was mad at her about something but what was it again? On Ash Wednesday she could not get ashes because she wasn't Catholic but she went to mass anyway and prayed upon her knees for forty days and nights (plus Sundays, which were *in addition to* the forty days and nights, a fact she found divinely sneaky) of strength, and afterward she checked into the Sleep Inn. A dive, but it was Lent, she told herself, not a vacation.

So here she is. The first day of Lent is a day of fasting and she is going to do this right, so she doesn't eat and she skips daytime TV, which had always struck her as a form of gluttony anyway. She opens her planner to look at all she will miss in her family's lives. Orchestra concert, end of basketball season, several soccer practices and the first game, report cards and conferences, young author's night, party with her husband's colleagues, wedding anniversary. Who will take the pictures, she wonders. Who will read the young author stories? Who—she cracks herself up on this one— will send her anniversary flowers? The children will eat processed school lunches every day, and what if one of them gets sick? *Give it up*, says a voice, though no one is there. *Go home.* Her stomach rumbles. She'll just lie down for a bit.

At 6 p.m. she awakes. The day is (technically) over! Now she can eat, as long as it's not meat. She goes to the bathroom, spritzes her hair, freshens her makeup (why not?), and walks next door to Hooters. The only other restaurant in walking distance is Wendy's, but she doesn't think they have fish. Not that she has to walk; she has her car and could go anywhere. Still, she is not someone you'd expect to see on the side of the road or cutting through a parking lot, so as she walks in the light rain on the gravel of the shoulder and over the curb, she is torn between absorbing the strange present moment being stared at by the occasional driver (she is forty; when is the last time that happened?), and pretending she is Christ forging her way through a sandstorm.

Outside Hooters, palm trees the color of highlighter pens; inside, a seat at the bar. What can I get you, asks a pair of boooobs dressed as an owl. (Is alcohol allowed during Lent?) Vodka tonic. Although the barflies stare (she is forty; when is the last time that happened?), the boooobs don't blanch. You want a menu? they say. Fish sandwich, fries, another vodka tonic. A light blue team plays a dark blue team in basketball on the large television. The barflies cheer whenever the dark blue team scores. I gave up my family, she tells the boooobs as they set the placemat and silverware before her, for Lent. There's worse reasons, the boooobs reply. I gave up mine for drugs.

The first Sunday of purple Lent. Hands clasp in purple prayer (must also give up nailbiting, evil vice). She can follow along, stand, sit, sing, mumble, pray (though it's just as boring as she predicted), but she cannot, in good conscience, eat the bread or drink the wine. It becomes its own temptation: to stand in line, to open palms, to open mouth, to receive the body and the blood. She could have gone where anyone off the street could take communion, but she prefers a place with standards. Dear Lord, she prays (for they are told to offer silent intentions), help me to think on You instead of my family. But she hasn't been thinking on her family at all, proof that the Lord knows your needs before you ask.

No, she reminds herself later, she is not giving up her whole life, just her family. But she finds upon consulting her planner that the only thing on tap for her in forty days and nights (plus Sundays) is book club. Several hours later it occurs to her that this gives her something else to do: read the book! She'd long ago dropped literary pretenses (Hello! Who's got that kind of time?) and focused instead on making distractingly delicious appetizers. Now in year three, in the wilderness, she would read. If she could just find where she'd written down the title.

March comes in like a cold wet sheep.

The boooobs are named Jaclyn. I wish I could do it over again, Jaclyn says. I'd get rid of the men not the kids. It all got tangled up—men, drugs, sex, money   and the kids got I don't know. I'd go back to them in a second but now they're older and don't want me. You're crazy, you know, Jaclyn tells her. You've got everything and you don't even know it. Believe me, I know it, she says. Why are you here then, asks Jaclyn. Why did Jesus go to the wilderness, she answers. Why did the Israelites? Moses? Elijah? I don't know, says Jaclyn, why? She doesn't exactly know either but is pretty sure it has something to do with divine providence.

But later that night: *You've got everything and you don't even know it. Believe me, I know it. You've got everything and you don't. Believe me, I know. You've got everything and. Believe me I.* Should go home. What is she doing? *I'd go back to my kids in a second. You're crazy. You've got. Your family, if it means so much, why are you call yourself a mother?*

A close-up car crackles gravel outside the room. Two doors open and shut. They know she's here alone and completely irresponsible. Putting herself at risk when her self is so valuable to the health and wellbeing of her family. Probably a couple barflies who've watched her and are now going to... One in particular always stares so (she is forty; when is the last time that happened?). At first she thought he was staring at Jaclyn, but even when the boooobs moved to a different part of the bar he was still looking her way. Not creepy though, just looking. Footsteps and low voices are approaching. The lamp she could grab and swing like a bat, the cord could strangle. She should be safe at home dreaming of the bus stop, of orders for the flower sale. *You call yourself a mother,* a voice says. *You call yourself a wife. Then why don't you go home?* I CALL MYSELF JENNIFER! she shouts, startling herself. The footsteps pass her room, fumble with another door, and grow silent. Jennifer, she says again, though quietly this time.

Jennifer finds that she rather likes reading the book club book. The main character is different from her in interesting ways (she lived during World War I, for instance, and is a nurse) but also similar (she struggles to express herself verbally, causing confusion and misunderstandings). Jennifer tells Jaclyn about the book. Jaclyn says she doesn't read much but that she might like to borrow it when Jennifer is finished. Something new, I suppose, why not, Jaclyn says in that way she has of talking half to Jennifer, half to herself, as she swabs the damp rag across the sticky varnished wood the way a painter might smear paint over a huge canvas. Jennifer thinks Jaclyn seems fairly pleased with the whole idea.

Friday night as Jimmy Buffett's voice falls down from the speakers singing about Saturday night the barfly who looked Jennifer's way even when Jaclyn's boooobs went elsewhere walks right over and asks if he can have a seat beside her. Better view of the game, he explains when she opens her mouth but can't quite formulate a reply. And just like that they are sitting next to each other. Jennifer faces forward, feels a strange prickle in the air along the right side of her body. He looks, she recalls from when he sat where she could see him, different from men in her neighborhood, from men at her children's schools. Those men wear shorter hair, ties, crisp Dockers. Not that this man isn't well-groomed. His shirts (like her husband's three-button golf shirts, but with Budweiser and Nascar logos) are always tucked into belted jeans, and he smells (she could tell just then when his body came toward hers and sat down) like evergreen and mint. The dark blue basketball team is on again, and even though she has seen him cheer for them every time they are on, she asks who he is rooting for. Just like that she says who instead of whom and ends a sentence with a preposition. He tells Jennifer about the dark blue team, and Jaclyn raises her eyebrows in what does not look like approval. The barfly's name is Matt.

Matt is from the class of two years before Jennifer at the rival high school. He has two daughters (between the ages of Jennifer's teen and tween) and they stay with him half the time. He pulls out his wallet to show pictures. Jennifer didn't have pictures with her (on purpose) and isn't even sure if she can talk about something she's given up. But one can talk about chocolate as long as one doesn't consume chocolate during Lent. So she describes her children in great detail and begins to miss them sharply. The next thing she knows she is crying and Matt is touching her shoulder. Jaclyn comes by with a drink napkin for her tears and takes the half-finished vodka tonic and pours it straight down the drain. Look what you've done, Jaclyn says to Matt. Go away! It's okay, Jennifer says, I'm okay, don't go. Go, Jaclyn says. Matt squeezes Jennifer's neck and says, I gotta get going anyway, I'll see you around.

But she doesn't see him around for two full weeks. Every morning she goes to mass and repents of the previous night's thoughts, which are not of cello performances and basketball games, but of the familiarly unfamiliar Matt, who looks at her even though she is forty, and who happened upon her like a movie scene set to high school's classic rock soundtrack. The priest speaks of temptation as if it were a person. Resist temptation, he says. The Israelites gave in. Be like Jesus. Let the spirit help. Blah, blah, blah.

I did it, Jaclyn says. I finished the book! Jaclyn noticed different things than Jennifer had. Jaclyn thought the main character was too weak even at the end. I really thought she was going to have this big triumph, Jaclyn says, but she just ended up where she started. But, Jennifer counters, she understood everything better and could be more, I don't know, intentional? It was realistic. Jaclyn says if she wanted realistic she would ask the people at the bar all their piss-sad tales. It seems like someone in a book should do better, she says. Otherwise the character might as well come right in here and drink it off.

The Doors are playing when Matt comes in, Light My Fire. Jaclyn is busy with the other side of the full bar, and Ryan the extra bartender refills Jennifer's vodka tonic three times. She tells Matt it is the Ides of March. Then she presses her nose to his ear and whispers, Beware! Which makes her laugh and take another sip of her drink. Her thoughts that week were of the shadow of him like the allegory of the cave. Now here he is in person, like Temptation the person, turned toward her, knees straddling her bar stool, saying, So, look, I don't really know your situation, and it's none of my business, but I like you. Do you, well, do you want to come over to my house? It's not far.

I like you too, she says.

Outside, between the doors and the cars, the palm trees blaze. Matt steps in front of Jennifer, puts his fingertips in the tender spot behind her jaw, like he is checking her pulse, which is thumping madly. And he just looks at her, he holds her gaze like they're in a staring contest. Everything about him is warm and brown like chocolate, and his lips have a slight smile like the tip of a Hershey's Kiss, like looking at her makes him happy. At last, at last he brings his face closer, still looking, still smiling. Their lips touch, softly, then less softly, then not soft at all. As if they've been starving and finally found a feast. Flames of orange and yellow flash behind his head. One of his arms presses her lower back, the other her upper. The flames, the heat. *Jennifer, Jennifer,* a voice other than the classic rock voice on the outside speakers, other than Matt, says, *Here I am, I know your sorrows.* Startled, Jennifer pulls away from Matt. The palm trees, she manages to say (though her lips want only to kiss), they're on fire. Matt looks at her like an object of study, then at the trees. See, she says, they're burning. Can't you see it? He kisses her again, softly, barely, and the flames are practically blue now with intensity. Oh god, can't you feel it, she says. Come on, he says, but when he walks to his car she does not follow him. He waits for a moment, turns on the car, waits again. Wait! Jennifer calls out after he finally drives off. For it is clear now that the highlighter palm trees are not charred and consumed, and so must not have been on fire after all.

The hours. They tug and pull. Her mind darts about like a pent up rodeo bull, but the clock catches her like a lasso, trips her feet, turns her over, ties her up, makes her wait. She prays for the time to pass more quickly. Dear Lord, she says, please. She opens her planner and there it is like a bible verse, *March 19: Daylight Savings.* Spring forward! And the Lord threw down a bolt from heaven and smote the hour.

It is the fifth Monday of Lent, and Jennifer awakens with a heavy heart. She is tired of Hooters; she is lonely at the Sleep Inn. And her family has a full week of activities that she can not attend. Grace, the youngest, is starting ballet classes, and who knows if anyone will remember to take her? Tony's basketball season is ending and soccer starts Thursday after school. Elaine's softball practices start today, and her orchestra concert is Thursday night. She plays first chair cello and will perform Jennifer's favorite, Vivaldi's Spring. Jennifer is lucky, blessed beyond belief, really, to have three healthy, smart, talented kids, and after months, years, of winding and winding and winding them up, she can, at these games and concerts, stop and simply let them play. She can watch them from an outsider's perspective in bleachers, fold-up chairs, and auditorium seats, and see a glimpse of the adults they will become—are becoming: for won't Elaine soon enough be married and raising two girls of her own? Won't Tony leave a corporate job behind so he can travel Europe with his recently divorced high school sweetheart? And won't Grace be splitting cells in a university laboratory? The only future Jennifer can't seem to see is her own. Well, at least this Thursday she won't have to decide between Elaine's concert and book club (not that there was a choice: of course the concert). And she has even read the book!

Where the hell have you been? Jennifer's entire book club is standing on the porch of Anne's house when she arrives. It is 6:37; she is only seven minutes late. At Kroger, she says, picking up a dish. The book club vultures in and clutches her arms. One takes the tray of meats and cheeses. Okay, they say, looking panicked, Don't panic. What? What is it? Jennifer panics. Listen, they say, he's doing fine now, do you hear us, he's *conscious*, but—. Oh god, but what? Jennifer feels their arms clutching harder, holding her up as her legs grow molten. It's Tony, they say. He hit his head on the goal post at soccer this afternoon and is in the hospital, but no one knew where you were. He's been asking for you. It's the side of his head at his ear, close to the temple, and it gave him a concussion but they kept him conscious the whole time so that's good, but now they're doing tests on his hearing. Oh god. Oh my god. Come on, they say. We're taking you to the hospital.

Don't cry, the book club says. Tim is with him. We're almost there. Hurry! Jennifer screams.

At last the line of trees breaks and the hospital appears on the hill to the right. Mercy, the sign says. The car slows and turns up the drive and to the drop-off zone. Jennifer rushes out of the car, through the huge sliding doors, past the gift shop, and toward the elevators, the book club at her side. They are in the green atrium of rocks and waterfall when Jennifer hears a voice. *Do not be afraid*, it says, *for I am with you*. Above the waterfall is a two-story-high mosaic cross, its dazzling colors alight with the late-day sun.

Come on, her book club says, tugging her arm. He's this way.

Jennifer's eyes are fixed on the enormous cross, the glittering reds, golds, purples, the sound of the voice. She feels small in comparison, but also strong. Stronger, in fact, than perhaps she has ever felt. She turns to face her book club. No, she says quietly. I'm not going to see him; take me back. The book club is incredulous. What do you mean? I mean take me back to Anne's, Jennifer says. I want to talk about the book. Are you crazy? What kind of mother? How could you? Their words hurt and she wavers. The voice returns and is calm: *Do not be afraid, for I am with you.* He is being cared for, Jennifer says, by excellent doctors at an excellent hospital. His father is with him. I'll see him on Easter.

Good for you, Jaclyn says, squeezing Jennifer's hand. You did good. Jennifer smiles. She did do good. Then she has an idea. Hey, she says to Jaclyn, it's supposed to be a gorgeous weekend. Do you want to rent a couple bikes and go for a long ride? Jaclyn steps back toward the cash register, holds out her arms and surveys her various body parts, as if she isn't quite sure they are up to the task. Finally she says, Yes?

Easter. Jennifer goes alone to the high mass, the one that starts in darkness on Saturday night. The heat of her candle warms her face when she holds it close. They're going crazy with the incense, the parading through the aisles and hoisting oversized candles and bibles, like actors in a junior high play. But she's come to like them, these men in robes. They put on their costumes and play their parts reliably, which ought to count for something. They are earnest, sometimes too earnest, about their roles as Fathers, but they occasionally, perhaps inadvertently, reveal a weariness about life and Fatherhood—a strange sense of relief about it being Lent, a church-sanctioned low-point—that Jennifer understands all too well. Father What's-His-Name spoke recently about daily sacrifices, about keeping up the good work. Or something. The point was that Jennifer saw herself parading through neighborhood streets in her minivan, preparing daily communion for her flock, ministering to her sick, like a priest. When the congregation had walked around the building waving palms on Palm Sunday (Jennifer had felt positively ridiculous), one of the priests-in-training followed the crowd around with a video camera like a proud parent. Yes, she relates to these priestly parents. But watching the robed men is, she would be the first to admit if someone asked (thought fat chance of that), Jennifer's deliberate strategy for averting the constant gaze of Mary, who, with her head bent at an angle that must be the mathematical calculation of motherhood, hovers and solemnly stares from the adjacent nave. Even now in the dark, Jennifer can feel Mary's eyes, like two candle flames, staring directly at her—just as they have through every mass. And Jennifer knows also that hers, Mary's, was the voice that soothed, that was with her this Lent. But she still finds it hard to meet that gaze.

Tomorrow the hotel housekeeper will find Jennifer's room an empty tomb. (Someone is reading the biblical story, and Jennifer thinks of her own resurrection.) The girls will think she is a ghost. Doubting Tony will touch her hands for proof. How's your head, Jennifer will ask. I'm sorry I couldn't be there, she'll tell him, but my spirit was with you. Yeah, he'll say, squeezing her hand. She will turn to her husband, speak his name. I buried the cat, he'll say. But he will be crying, right there on the lawn in front of kids and tulips. He will be crying because he knows as well as she that sometimes it is too much and other times it is too little, but in the end it is, they are, all and everything. She will place her palm on his moist cheek, and look from him to the children. I am with you always—Jennifer, like Jesus, will promise (here, now, she looks up at Mary and does not look away, she can almost feel herself ascending)—until the end of this world.

Acknowledgments

This book has been encouraged, inspired, and improved by so many people that it feels like a group effort. Many thanks to Shannon Cain, Lisa Bowden, and the staff at Kore Press for making this house of stories a home.

At the University of Cincinnati, Brock Clarke, Michael Griffith, and Jim Schiff were impossibly intelligent and generous, and their support seems to know no end. My fellow students turned into the best of comrades and friends (how else to explain the karaoke?). Special thanks to Kristin Czarnecki, Molly McCaffery, Sarah Domet, and Julie Gerk Hernandez, who, I keep pinching myself, lives near me once again. Thanks to Darrin Doyle and Kirsten Lunstrum for the kind words. I cherish my long-term friendships with Annette Eberhardt, Jen Bumgartner, Lisa Campbell, Meredith Miller, and Kimberly Kohus. I've been lucky to find a new home in Indiana, and I'm grateful to my energizing colleagues and inspiring students at Indiana University South Bend.

Special thanks: to my mom, Janice Patton, for first placing books into my hands and heart; to my dad, Gary Ervick, who taught me to throw a spiral and believe in myself; to my beautiful sister, Darcy, for making me seem smarter and funnier than I am; and to my brother, Dane, my go-to guy for philosophical conversations. To Pat and Christian and Travis, who've multiplied the love - and the height - of the family. To Karen Parker and in memory of Bruce. To my grandparents again. And to BJ, who I fell for on the first day of seventh grade (and a thousand times since); and to Monte, my best girl.

Very few of the persons listed above will be surprised to learn that writing these paragraphs made me cry.

Many of these stories previously appeared in the following journals:

Redivider, Santa Monica Review, Bellingham Review, Portland Review, Western Humanities Review, Amoskeag, Sycamore Review, Indiana Review, Nidus, the George Washington Review, and *Image.* My thanks to those editors, whose yesses kept me going.

The italicized sections in "Maugham's Head" are from W. Somerset Maugham's *The Moon and Sixpence.*

About the Author

Kelcey Parker's stories have been published in various edited collections and in journals such as *Third Coast, Redivider, Bellingham Review, Santa Monica Review, Western Humanities Review, Indiana Review, Portland Review, Sycamore Review,* and twice in *Image,* where she was featured as Artist of the Month in November 2009. She is a contributing writer for the *Novel & Short Story Writer's Market,* and has also published book reviews and academic essays. She received a Ph.D. in Creative Writing and Literature from the University of Cincinnati, and currently lives with her husband and daughter in Northern Indiana, where she is an assistant professor at Indiana University South Bend. Her virtual home is www.kelceyparker.com

About the Press

As a community of literary activists devoted to bringing forth a diversity of voices through works that meet the highest artistic standards, Kore Press publishes women's writing that deepens awareness and advances progressive social change.

Kore has been publishing the creative genius of women writers since 1993 in Tucson, Arizona, to maintain an equitable public discourse and establish a more accurate historic record.